# When Forever Fails

*When Forever Fails*
Copyright © 2018 by Shelly Leanne Sharp

Published in the United States of America
ISBN Paperback: 978-1-947765-55-9
ISBN eBook: 978-1-947765-56-6

All rights reserved. No part of this publication may be reproduced, stored in a retrieval system or transmitted in any way by any means, electronic, mechanical, photocopy, recording or otherwise without the prior permission of the author except as provided by USA copyright law.

No lines, parts, and quotations were taken from other books or any previous publications.

The opinions expressed by the author are not necessarily those of ReadersMagnet, LLC.

ReadersMagnet, LLC
10620 Treena Street, Suite 230 | San Diego, California, 92131 USA
1.619.354.2643 | www.readersmagnet.com

Book design copyright © 2018 by ReadersMagnet, LLC. All rights reserved.
*Cover design by Ericka Walker*
*Interior design by Shieldon Watson*

# When Forever Fails

## Shelly Leanne Sharp

READERSMAGNET, LLC

*Dedicated to those who have served, are serving, or will serve.
Thank you all for your sacrifice to keep us all free. You are heroes!
To Jesus, who was the ultimate sacrifice for us. Thank you
for loving us so much that you would die for us.
Also dedicated to my family, friends, and loved ones.
To Destinee and Nathan, Rissa, Haley, ZayLea, and Adi.
You will always be my babies. To my children from other mothers
as well. To my parents. Thanks for putting up with me
all these years. I was very blessed to have you guys.
I could not have asked for better parents.
I love you all! To Matthew-I am praying for you
sweetie. You were a little brat growing up but now
you are definitely my hero. Love you kiddo.*

# Prologue

"Hello," Hope Smith said sleepily into the telephone receiver. The clock on the wall showed 3:26 AM. She knew who would be on the phone before she ever answered it. Only one person would call that late.

"Hey Goober, what's up? How's it going? How have you been lately and how are the girls?" All it took was the sound of his voice and Hope felt her lips turn upward into a smile. How long had it been since she had heard the sound of that voice? That was the voice that had helped her get through the roughest times in her life. That voice was the one that had been on the other end of the line when she was breaking down during her divorce. That was the voice of the best friend that she had ever known. That voice had sung her a beautiful song letting her know much he cared about her during his leave, the voice that had told her that he loved her when they were making love the first time and the voice was also the one that had broken her heart when he told her that he had to leave to go back. That voice belonged to Trey McDaniel.

"We are doing good. How have you been? Where are you at these days?"

"You won't believe me when I tell you. We left out about a month ago and I am now in Japan."

"That's crazy. You are so far from home! I knew it had been a long time since you called. I always know when you are at sea when you don't call me for awhile."

"Yea, you lost a lot of sleep when I was in Guam. You heard from me almost every night when I was there. I've missed hearing your sleepy voice since we have been out to sea. What's new with you, your kids, and with our hometown? Any good gossip? Gosh I miss that place. I also miss you and the girls."

"Awe, we miss you too. Ugh, you know that nothing big ever happens here. Same old town, different day. The girls are getting big. Desirae told me to tell you hi the next time that you call though and that she misses you. Kelsey is now potty trained. I am so proud of them both. How's Japan? I'm sure it is a much more exciting place. I wish that I could go around and see the world like you do. I get sick of being here. I get tired of everyone knowing everything I do before I even do it. Oh the joys of living in a small town your entire life," she said sarcastically.

"Truthfully, I would trade places with you in a heartbeat. It would be kind of nice for people to know you instead of everyone you see to walk past you like you are not there. I am sick of the traveling. The only people I know are the guys I work with and they get old after rooming with them day in and day out. I just want to get somewhere and settle down again. Wish I was there with you right now. I got your letters. They are all that keeps me going sometimes. The sea sure gets lonely. Being under the water makes it worse. We were under the water over a month this time. I get so sick of it."

"I wish that you were here too. I miss hanging out and having fun together." More than anything, she missed the feeling of his warm arms wrapped around her, holding her tightly to him. She missed the feel of his warm, soft lips against hers, and his hand holding hers. She could not let him know that though because she would lose his friendship and she could not bear that thought. "We sure had a good time the last time you came to town."

"Yea we did. I don't regret that leave at all. It was the best time of my life. Well I have to let you go now. I have to get back to post. It was great to hear your voice again. Give the girls a big hug from me and let them know that I love and miss them. Sorry I woke you up but you know how it goes, our time is so different that sometimes that is the only chance I can call."

"Trey for the thousandth time, don't ever be sorry. I would rather get drug out of bed at 3am than not to hear from you. You can call me anytime day or night. It means the world to me to hear your voice. I look forward to hearing more from you soon."

"That's why I adore you so much, you don't care what time I call. Talk to you soon. Remember, when you hear the wind blowing in your ear or feel the warmth of the sun on your skin, I'm there with you in my heart. Remember that when you look up at the moon, I will be staring at the same one. Take care, Hope. See you tonight in my dreams."

"I know because you are in my dreams too," she said, her voice beginning to break. "Talk to you later." She knew it that her voice would be ratting her out soon if she did not get off the phone.

"Bye beautiful. Sweet dreams."

"Bye bye."

She placed the phone back on the hook and the tears came at once. She did not understand. He just told her that when he had came down for leave, it had been the best time of his life. They were the best days of hers too so why did they have to break up? After he left to go back to the Navy, he had quit talking to her for about 6 weeks so she had written him a letter telling him that she was sorry that he had gotten upset and told him that she wanted and needed their friendship more than ever and could not bare to lose him. She told him that she would rather just have him as a friend than not to have him at all. That was the hardest thing that she had ever had to do but she would rather have him as a friend than lose him. She was not sure what had caused him to quit talking to her-the miles or the stress of being in a relationship. At first she thought that he must be at sea until she had spoken to his father, who told her that he had heard from him that day. She needed that friendship so she said goodbye to the relationship. He was her rock.

She had met Trey when she was in the eighth grade and he was in the seventh. Throughout the years, they had become friends and had always been there for each other. When she was 15, she had gotten a boyfriend that had become very jealous of her guy best friend and had told him that if he talked to her anymore, he would kick his butt. She and Trey had quit speaking for awhile after that but eventually she had put her foot down with her boyfriend and told him that Trey had been there for her before he ever entered her life and that Trey was going to stay. Trey had green eyes, was 5 foot 8, and had the biggest smile. He had asked Hope to go out with him when he was 13 and she was 14 but her parents did not allow her to date so she had told him no. He finally talked her into it and she said yes but ended up breaking up with him after one day. He was very sweet to her though and even brought a rose to school for her. She just did not want to make her dad upset or disrespect his rules. Plus she was not into him, not like that when she was that age. Something had happened over time though. He had been the one that had kept her from drowning when she was going through her divorce, he had been the one that had talked her through it and kept her from losing her mind, and he had been the one that had treated her the way that she had always wanted to be treated. Somehow, someway he had gone from being the best friend to being the only one that she wanted to be with. When her husband Seth had been unfaithful, she fell head over heels in love with her best friend. She had been faithful in her marriage but Seth was not. He had cheated on her and Trey had caught his wife in bed with another man. He had gone from her best friend to everything she had ever wanted in a man. It was strange because they both had been cheated on at almost the same time and had helped each other through their darkest hours.

When Seth left her, Trey had flew in to Texas all the way from Hawaii to see her when she needed him the most. She had fallen in love with him and they had crossed a line from best of friends to the best thing that ever happened for her. Now after that line had been crossed, she had to step back over that line and be just friends so she will not have to lose him. How do you do that? How do you go back after you have already fallen? How do you say goodbye to the best thing you ever had, the greatest love you will ever know and go back to being just friends? She was not ready to close this chapter in her life but if she didn't she would have to lose him for good and could not do that. As much as she needed him and loved him, she had to let go of those feelings at least for now.

# Chapter 1

## *They Meet*

It was the day of her 15th birthday party. She had numerous girls over for a slumber party. They had decided to prank call several people from their school just for the fun of it and Chasity Gates had mentioned that they prank call her cousin. They called Trey and asked him numerous questions, pretending to be a survey company. They kept asking him questions about if he wanted to be in the military and then finally ended the call with the question, what would you do if this is a prank call.

He said "Well, I would probably laugh. Who is this and you got me." Hope laughed and told him who she was and that they had called because his cousin Chasity Gates had mentioned that it would be funny and he would take it well. He laughed and that was the first interaction they ever had. This was in September, 1991 but that Monday at school, he found her and introduced himself. She laughed and asked how he felt about the military and its policies. He grinned at her and told her that truthfully he had considered going into the military after he graduated.

"How did you know who I was?"

"I looked at my step brother's yearbook and found you since you prank called me to find out who you were," he said smiling.

"Oh cool. It is nice to meet you. Honestly I didn't have a clue who you were until you introduced yourself just now. I've heard of you but I never really knew who you were."

"Well, you have my number now and have prank called me and I only think it is fair that you give me yours in return so I will have the chance to call you or prank you back."

"Fair enough," she told him. From that moment on, they talked on the phone all the time. Not a day went by without them talking on the phone. When he asked her out, she explained to him that her parents did not allow her to date or have a boyfriend. That made him sad and she felt bad so she agreed to go out with him. He had always been sweet to her and she didn't want to hurt his feelings. He showed up at school the next day holding a pink rose from his mother's garden in a yellow plastic cup full of water. She decided at that point that she had to break up with him because they would end up getting caught and she would get into trouble for having a boyfriend. Plus she was not into him and did not want to hurt him if he got too serious. He was upset but they agreed to be friends and that they became. They would stay up all night at times, talking on the phone about everything and nothing. They talked about their brothers, dogs, school, and their activities they liked.

One night, they were talking on the phone and she heard him start breathing funny. He had fallen asleep on the phone with her. She thought it was sweet and the sound of his breathing was relaxing so she laid the phone next to her and listened to that until she also fell asleep with the phone next to her. He then made it a joke that she was technically the first person that he had ever slept with since they both fell asleep on the phone with each other.

They danced with each other at her 8th grade dance and spent several hours at Six Flags together during a band concert, riding rides and having fun. He was truly one of the best friends that she could ever ask for but friendship was all she wanted from him. They stopped at a restaurant on the way home and he got her a red balloon filled with helium and she was hanging onto it. A friend of hers asked if she could hold it for a minute and accidentally let it go and it flew out the window. He would give Hope a hard time about that for years to come. He always told her that she let his balloon go. Teasing each other and giving each other a hard time was always a big factor in their friendship. They enjoyed that.

Several months later, she met Seth at her friend Mitzi Boggs' pool party and things changed between her and Trey for awhile. She had known who Seth was for a long time and had always had a crush on him. He had flirted with her at that party and she really liked him. He ended up asking her out and she had told him yes in a heartbeat. By that time, she was 15 and her parents didn't mind if she had a boyfriend anymore.

She and Seth started spending all their time together and when Trey would call her, Seth would get mad. He would tell her that he felt like Trey was disrespecting him because she was his girlfriend and not Trey's. He told her that he felt like Trey called her too many times and that made him mad. She explained that Trey was just her friend and that he didn't have anything to worry about because he was harmless and she only had eyes for Seth. He didn't care. He wanted to stop that friendship. He had never allowed any of his girlfriends in the past to talk to another guy. She did not realize at that point that he was starting to show how possessive he really was. She did not have any clue that was just a preview of what was yet to come. Anyway, she didn't want to lose her best friend so she would tell Trey when Seth was there that Seth was at her house and she would call him back later so that Seth would not get mad.

Seth answered her phone once when she had gone to the restroom and was rude to Trey. "Trey, this is her boyfriend and I do not like you calling her. She is my girlfriend and if you call her again, I will kick your butt. I am not going to put up with someone calling my girl all the time." She had come out of the bathroom as he was hanging up asked who he was talking to. "I just had a heart to heart with your friend Trey. I don't think he will be calling quite as often. I think it is crap that he calls here so much if he is just a friend."

"I don't understand why he bothers you so much. He is harmless and he would never hurt a flea. He has been my friend for years and we have never even kissed."

"Yea but he was your boyfriend once and that is not cool. He would kiss you in a heartbeat if you would let him so don't give me that. I don't talk to any of my ex girlfriends."

"He was my boyfriend for less than a day. I let him go because I just wanted to be friends. I don't want to just be friends with you though. I want to be your girlfriend so please don't let him bother you. I just don't understand why it bothers you. He is a good friend of mine but he is not going to come between us ok."

"It is a respect thing. He don't respect me."

"I disagree with you. He always asks about you and said that he is happy that I have a boyfriend."

"Sure he asks about me. He is trying to get on my good side but he don't mean it. You will see, if that little worm ever has a chance, he will be with you in a heartbeat and not care at all about what I have to say. I guarantee you that if anything happened to us, he would be there in the shadows, ready to swoop in and take you himself. I just don't want another guy after my girl ok? Will you forgive me for wanting you all to myself?" He leaned in and hugged and kissed her, which usually got her to drop the subject when she really wanted him to understand something. It worked.

The next day, she had apologized to Trey for the way that her boyfriend had talked to him. "Trey, I am sorry. He don't understand us. He is not friends with any of his exs so he don't understand that girls and guys can get along and not be in a relationship with one another. I'm sorry. Are you mad at me?"

"Look Hope, I don't want to fight your boyfriend. He is a big guy and I don't need any trouble. I will back off while you are with him. I don't need to get into a fight." He pulled away. He did not Seth to feel like he was disrespecting him and he sure did not want to get into a fight with him. He went on with his life and she went on with hers without each other in it. He always missed their telephone conversations and he missed his friend, but he figured that she would eventually come back around. He also was scared that if he talked to her that Seth would be meant to her for talking to him. She also missed Trey. He had been a great friend to her and it broke her heart that her boyfriend's jealousy had drove them apart. She barely got to speak to him for over a year because what Seth had done. Her parents bought her a car one day and she seen Trey walking home from school one day so she pulled over.

"Want a ride Trey?"

"Not really, it will make Seth mad."

"I don't care. It is hot and the car has a good air conditioner. He has been mean to me lately anyway and I need to talk to someone about it. Please get in and let me take you home."

He reluctantly got into the car and she took him home where they got out and talked over a soda. She apologized to him for allowing a boyfriend to come between them and when she left, she went straight to Seth's house and told him that she was through being told what to do and that Trey was there before he was and that they were going to be friends no matter what he said. He was very mad and told her that she made him look like an idiot but promised not to hurt Trey when she threatened to break up with him if he hurt him. She started giving Trey rides home from that point on so he would not have to walk and sometimes they would stay at his house and have a soda after school. If Seth was around, Trey tried to steer clear of him because he did not trust him.

When she went to prom, she went up and hugged Trey who had brought a girl into the prom that had gotten into the door and danced with everyone but Trey. As Seth was dancing with Hope, he saw the sad look on Trey's face and told her. "Trey looks really upset. I think you should go ask him to dance. I kind of feel sorry for him since that girl did that to him."

"Will you be mad?"

"No, he is your friend and I accept that now. I think I am going to dance with Mitzi. I am sure you will not care if I dance with one of your best friends. Mitzi would never do anything with me anyway. She is too pretty and would not be seen with someone like me."

"Of course not. I trust you and Mitzi. Have fun." So she went up to Trey and asked him to dance with her.

"It depends. Is Seth going to rearrange my face if we dance?"

"Actually, this was his idea. He hates what happened to you tonight so he told me to come ask you to dance with me."

"I'm glad that guy finally quit hating me. I never did anything to him."

"I know, he can be jealous from time to time." They danced a slow song and then walked off the dance floor together, where he hung out with, talked, and laughed with her and Seth some. Then when "You Have the Right To Remain Silent" by Perfect Stranger came on, he asked Seth for permission to dance with her and Seth and him were ok with each other for the time being. Seth realized that he actually liked the guy.

As the time went on, she ended up marrying Seth and they had 2 babies. She truly loved Seth with everything in her heart. Trey went off to the military and they lost contact for years. At one point, she ran into Trey's father when she was working and asked about him. She introduced herself and he smiled and told her that he remember hearing Trey talk about her a lot when he was younger. He told her that he had been in the Navy for several years and told her that he was stationed at Hawaii. He told her that it was sometimes hard for him being so far away from home and that he loved to hear from friends and family. He gave her Trey's phone number so she could call him to say hello. She didn't know how Seth would take it but she really wanted to talk to Trey again. She had missed her little buddy over the years.

She thought about whether or not she should call Trey. Seth had been very cruel to her over the years and their relationship had really gone downhill. She had a gut feeling that he was cheating but could not prove it. The best thing that they ever did though was have their beautiful babies. Desirae had blonde hair and beautiful blue eyes. She was the spitting image of her daddy. Kelsey took after her mama with the same brown hair and brown eyes. She would look into that little girls face and see herself when she was little. They both had their own little personalities but that made them who they were. She loved those babies more than life itself. She would do anything in the world for either one of them.

The next day, she told Seth that she wanted to talk. "I ran into Trey's father last night and he gave me his phone number. Do you care if I call him to see how he is doing? His dad said that he gets homesick so I wanted to surprise him."

"Seriously? Where is he at? Why didn't you just ask his dad how he was doing?"

"I did and his dad said that he gets lonely and likes to hear from his friends and family. He is in Hawaii so he isn't a threat. I may never even see him again."

"Hawaii huh? Yea go ahead. I don't care. You will probably never see him again as long as he is over there so he isn't really a threat anymore. Don't talk too long though because we can't afford a expensive phone bill. You talk to Mitzi sometimes and you never talk too long so make sure you do that with him too ok?"

"I won't. You won't be mad?"

"Nah, he is your best friend so go ahead and knock yourself out. Plus it's Hawaii. That's halfway around the world. He would have to fly to get to you so like I said, he isn't a threat. He is not as attractive as me," he said chuckling. "I don't have to worry about him at all." She just shook her head at his cockiness. Secretly, she had always thought that Trey was adorable but was not going to disclose that information to Seth.

She picked the phone up and dialed the number that his father had given her. She heard that familiar voice on the answering machine. "Hey, this is Trey. Leave me a name and number and I will get back with you soon."

"Hey Trey, I don't know if you remember me because it has been years, but this is Hope Smith from high school. I saw your dad at my job yesterday and he knew we used to be friends so he gave me your number. I would love to hear from you if you get the opportunity to call me back. Have a great day." She left her phone number then hung the phone up.

"Did you already talk to him?" Seth asked.

"No, but I left him a message so we will see if he calls back. Thanks for understanding that I want to see how he is and that he is one of my best friends. It's been several years since we have spoken to him."

"As long as you don't run off with him and you are in love with me and not him, we will be just fine. I don't see that happening though. You would never be attracted to someone like him after you have been with me. He never was a looker. I would say you are not pretty enough for him but the little worm always had the hots for you. I will never understand why but I guess ugly attracts ugly." He was always putting her down like that. She loved him but hated that about him.

"That's rude but would never happen. I only love you. I have never looked at him as anything but a friend."

"Sweetheart, I love you and I don't want us to argue anymore. I'm sorry I have been a jerk lately. I love you and our daughters so much." He seemed so convincing at times but she knew the real him.

"I don't know why. You always tell me how ugly I am Seth. How would you like it if I told you that? You used to tell me that I was beautiful. I'm sorry I don't want to fight. Love you too, hon." She truly loved Seth but some of the ways that he treated her made her question if he really loved her. She kissed him bye and he left for work. He would sometimes call her bad names and tell her that she was stupid. He had her convinced that if they ever broke up, nobody else would ever want or love her because she had two kids and was not desirable anymore. She had gained some weight and he told her that he was not even attracted to her so why would anyone else be? She believed every single bad word that he had called her throughout the years and thought badly of herself after all the years of mental abuse. She wished more than anything that he would change but so far that hadn't happened. He would stay out sometimes for hours at a time, if he came home at all. He liked to party and left her alone to care for the kids.

Instead of getting better things had just gotten worse. She believed that if she was a better wife, mom, and lover he would treat her better because he had convinced her that everything was her fault. She always apologized for everything because he made her believe that everything wrong was her fault. He used to be nice. Somehow he had become someone that even he could not stand but she thought that was her fault also. He never helped her with the kids because he felt that was her job even though she worked more hours per week than he did. She was the only one that would cook or clean but she tried her best not to complain because he always told her that was what wives were supposed to do. Sometimes she felt like a slave in her own house but she just tried to keep going. She started picking up the mess that the girls had made and cleaned the kitchen when she heard the phone ring.

She picked up the phone and said hello.

"What do you mean you don't know if I would remember you or not. How could I forget the girl that I call my best friend to this day?"

"Oh my Gosh, Trey, how are you?"

"I am good, enjoying Navy life but I am so ready to come home. I miss everyone there in Breckenridge. Gosh it has been years since I have been back. Hopefully I will get to go home on leave soon."

"That would be cool. I bet you do miss everyone. Have you seen anyone lately?"

"Yea my mom flew here to see me for a few days then had to go home and my brother came to see me once when I had been here for about two months, but other than that, no. I have run into a couple of guys we went to school with though. They are both enlisted." He told her the names of the guys that he had seen.

"Wow, that's cool. At least you have seen a few people from home. I bet it gets lonely out there."

"You have no clue. All I want to do is come home for just a few days. I want to see everyone. So, how is married life? How is Seth and your daughters?" She got him up to date on the home situation, leaving out the mental abuse that Seth put her through on a daily basis. She didn't want anyone to know how bad he was. She didn't even let her mom and dad know and they just lived down the road from her. She was afraid everyone would look at her as a failure if they knew.

"What about you? Any girlfriend or wife yet?"

"Nope, it's just me. I sometimes wish that I had one but it hasn't happened for me yet. I stay too busy to get one of those."

"I understand. Don't worry, the right one will come along. Just be patient."

"I am. No big deal. So, do you guys still live in that same house?"

"Yes, we do. We have been here for years now. We are buying it so we don't plan on leaving anytime soon. I hate to move anyway."

"Cool, hey I can't stay on the phone. I have to leave for work in about five minutes but I want to get your address and give you mine so we can write each other. I would love it if you would send me a picture of you with your daughters. I've never even seen the baby. She was not born yet when I left. I bet they have gotten big," he told her.

"Sure writing would be cool. They are so beautiful. I can't believe how fast they are growing." She gave him her address and he gave his to her. They said their goodbyes and hung up. Wow, it was so great hearing each other's voice again. They had missed each other terribly but hadn't realized it until they heard each other's voices again. About a week later, she had written him a long letter and mailed it off. After she got home from the post office, Seth told her that Trey had called her and said that he was going to call her after he got off work that night.

"How was he?"

"I didn't make small talk. I'm sure that he was fine though. You know I never have been much of a fan. Now that he has your phone number, this is not going to be a habit, is it? He won't call you every freaking day now, will he?"

"No, I'm sure that he could not afford to call everyday." He kissed her goodbye and left to go work on his uncle's truck with him. About 2 hours later, there was a knock at the door. She opened it.

"Surprise Goober!"

"What are you doing here?" She asked throwing her arms around his neck. "I can't believe you are here!"

"When we spoke last week, I knew that they were transferring me to Florida but before I went there, they were going to let me have a weeks leave but I didn't want to tell you that because it would ruin your surprise. I was already planning on stopping by to see you but then when I got your call, I thought it would be cool to keep it a surprise."

"It is so good seeing you, Trey. Come in. Seth told me that you had called and that you would call me back tonight after you got off work."

"I didn't want to tell Seth I was in town because I was scared that he would accidentally ruin the surprise. I am so glad that you called me. I have missed you throughout the years."

"I bet your dad is happy you are in town."

"Truthfully, he hasn't seen me yet. I am surprising everyone with this visit. You were my first stop."

"Seriously?"

"Yeppers."

"Hey mama, who's that?" Desirae asked from behind her.

"That's Desirae? She has grown. Hey sweetie, I am your mom's friend, Trey. Wow. She isn't a baby anymore. Where's Kelsey? You sure are beautiful Princess. You were just a baby the last time that I saw you, Sweetheart. Are you sure that this big girl is Desirae? I can't believe it."

"Yep, Desirae is a big girl now. Kelsey is taking a nap. Come on, you can peak in at her."

"Thank you Mr. Trey for calling me beautiful Princess."

"Can I have a hug Desirae?"

She reached her little arms out and allowed him to pick her up and give her a hug. "Come on, let's go back and look at your sister. We have to be really quiet so that we don't wake her up." Hope led him to her daughters' room and he peeked into the baby bed to see her sleeping one year old. "She is so beautiful. She looks just like you," he whispered.

"Yea, I can't deny her," she said smiling at her baby. They walked out of the room and sat down at the table to talk. "So are you glad that you are going to Florida?"

"Yes I am. I love Hawaii. It is paradise but it is so small. You can drive from one end of the island to the other in about an hour. It is the most beautiful place but I am glad to be back in Texas. I am even happier to be back in Breckenridge. I have missed everyone here so bad. It gets lonely on the submarine."

"Well, Breckenridge is glad to have you back. You hungry? I will make supper and you can eat with us."

"I can't. I will go to Dad's house shortly and I will just eat with him. He is going to flip out when he sees me. Don't tell him that I came by to see you first. He will get mad at me because he is my dad," he said grinning. They talked for about an hour when the baby woke up and she went to change her and get her out of her baby bed. Desirae had parked herself up in Trey's lap and was asking him questions and showing him how smart she was. When she was getting the baby, Seth returned and saw Trey holding his daughter.

"What are you doing back? I thought you were in Hawaii," he asked, feeling his anger coming on.

"Hello Seth. I am on leave and wanted to surprise everyone." Trey got up and went to Seth and extended his hand to shake Seth's.

"Hawaii my butt. Did my wife know that you were coming in this week?" he asked, sounding annoyed. Seth took his hand and squeezed it really hard when he went to shake it.

"I have been in Hawaii and just flew into DFW today for a leave before they transfer me to Florida. I rented a car and drove to Breckenridge. I wanted to see Hope, you, my dad, brothers, step parents, a couple more friends, and then I will drive to Houston to see my mom. I will stay with her most of my leave. Nobody knew I was coming. I haven't even told my dad."

"When did you get in and was Hope the first person you came to see?" Seth asked, allowing his anger to show.

"Well, I went to see my dad and he was not home," he fibbed. "He is probably still working. I figured that I would come on over and see you and Hope really quick then go back to Dad's to see if he was home yet. I'm trying to make the best of my time while I am here and won't have that long to be here A week is a very short time to see everyone that I want to see."

"Wouldn't your dad take off when his son comes down for a leave since he hasn't seen you in a long time?"

"I am going to surprise him too. He does not know that I am here yet," he repeated himself.

"Oh, well you may want to go see him soon so he don't get upset. I would be ticked off if my son went to see a stupid girl before he came home to see me." Trey could tell that he was not wanted and was not welcome at that point so he figured when Hope came back into the kitchen, he would excuse himself quickly so Seth would not get too upset and take it out on her after he left. It made him very mad that Seth had referred to her as a stupid girl. She had been pretending that things were ok between her and Seth but Trey could see right past her act. He could see the pain in her eyes and could hear it in her voice. She could fake it all she wanted to but he had known her for years and knew her well. He also knew the kind of person Seth was and knew that typically he was a pretty mean guy. When she came out of the bedroom, he held Kelsey for a minute then told Hope that he had to leave to go see if his dad was home.

"It was good seeing all of you," he told them.

"It was great seeing you too. You take care and drive careful when you leave," she told him.

"I will, I promise. See y'all later. Later girls. Bye Seth." He stood up and hugged Hope bye but didn't miss the fact that Seth was glaring at him from behind her. He looked at Seth and reached out to take his hand. Seth quickly took his hand and squeezed it really hard again. Trey said bye and walked out. He had not gotten to the end of the sidewalk when Seth started in.

"What the heck Hope? You can't tell me that you didn't know that he was coming in for a leave. Why did you allow him to hold my daughters? That's crap Hope. He had no right holding my kids."

"Seth, I did not know that you would care. He had held Desirae before and he would never do anything to hurt them. Why are you so upset? I don't understand why you are mad."

"Where's supper Hope? You should have been cooking supper instead of entertaining your stupid ex boyfriend."

"Seriously Seth? He is my friend, nothing more. Why do we have to go back to you being jealous? I thought we were past all this crap."

"I'm not jealous of him, I just don't like him. I can't stand him coming over to see my wife and holding my kids. Then I have to see you hug him. You might as well have had sex with him the way you throw yourself at him," he told her.

"Cook your own supper Seth. I am not going to stand here and listen to you accuse me of doing something that I would never do. You can be such a jerk at times. I'm going to my parents house. A hug is nothing like sex. You are the only one that I have ever been with so please stop saying that."

"Yea, right, you might as well go find your little boyfriend, slut. I can't believe that I married someone like you. You are a fat worthless piece of crap. You are easy. You are a slut. I always had beautiful, skinny girls and I settled for you. I would have never married you if you had not gotten yourself knocked up. Sometimes I hate you for becoming who you are."

"I can't believe that you would call me that. You are the only person that I have ever slept with in my entire life. I have never even kissed anyone else. I am sorry your life is so bad Seth. I am sorry that I got fat." She walked out of the room, picked up both of her kids, and left. The apology was sincere. She always believed everything was her fault. After she was out the door, he grabbed a stack of plates and threw them across the room, watching them all shatter into little pieces. Then he grabbed his keys and sped off to McDonald's to grab a bite to eat.

She and her kids ate supper with her parents that night. She did not let anything on to her parents that they were having problems. She tried to hide that from everyone. He didn't come home until late. She cleaned up the glass when she got home so that Desirae would not step on the shattered pieces and cut herself and put her babies to bed. She apologized to him when he got home, thinking that once again, it must be her fault. "I love you Seth. I hope you can forgive me. I didn't mean to upset you or call you jealous. I really did not know that he was coming. I'm sorry. I can see how that must have upset you since I did not tell you. I am also sorry that I have gained weight and am not as good as the girls before me."

"Whatever. Don't talk to me, fat cow. He would not want you anyway anymore. You have let yourself go. You are enormous and you are lousy in bed. You are not good for anything. I hate you."

She rolled over and cried herself to sleep again. This had become the normal in their life lately. She was getting used to him cursing her and calling her horrible names and crying herself to sleep.

About 4 days later, she was working and Trey came through the drive through and introduced her to Danica. I want to bring her by your house today after you get off, I have great news.

"Sure. Try to come by between 4-10 ok," She hated to ask him to come by while Seth was working but did not want to fight him anymore. It just was not worth it to fight with him.

"Ok sounds good." When he came by her house, he told her that he had met Danica when visiting his mother in Houston and they were going to get married in Florida. She was going home with him to Florida.

"Wow, don't you think you guys are jumping in really quickly?"

"You don't understand. Danica is the one. I have never met anyone like her before and I know that this is going to work out."

"Wonderful. I'm happy for both of you then." She hugged them both then he told her that he had to leave to go introduce her to his dad.

When he left, she was so happy for him. He was such a sweetheart and deserved to be happy. He deserved a great girl and being with someone for a long time did not guarantee a happy marriage. Just look at her and Seth, they had dated for 5.5 years before getting married and neither one of them were happy. She decided just to be excited for him and that she truly was.

# Chapter 2

## Trouble in Paradise

Life went on as it always does. The longer she stayed with Seth, the more she realized that she didn't know if she could stay with him much longer. Mitzi had came by to see her and Seth one day and had brought her boyfriend Chuck. When they were there, Seth had popped off and degraded Hope and the babies. At that point, Chuck stood up and told Mitzi "Mitzi, it's time to go. Thank you for having us over Hope. Supper was wonderful." He turned and glared at Seth who just smiled at him. About two weeks later, Mitzi saw her at her job and told her that she was sorry they had to leave that night but that Chuck had told her that if he had to listen to Seth talk to Hope like that one more time, he was going to fight him and he did not want to disrespect Hope like that in her home.

"Hope, Chuck said that you are a really great woman and don't deserve to have to go through that. He also said that you are a beautiful woman and could do much better than Seth. I have never seen Chuck so mad in my life. I just thought that you should know."

"Mitzi, Chuck and I have never been close and in a way, he is a stranger. How is it that a complete stranger can see that I am an idiot and I can't see it? I don't even understand why I stay." she told her.

"I don't know Hope. I am going to go so you can sit there and think about it. I love you and am always here for you but you deserved to hear the truth." With that, Mitzi walked off and left her with nothing but her thoughts. Hope felt like she had just been slapped by reality. Wow a stranger could see that he was treating her wrong but she kept putting up with it. Those few words from Mitzi said more to her than she could have said with an all day long conversation. She just hung her head and decided that she needed to just let it go. She had started going to nursing school to try to better their lives and Seth resented her for that. He thought that she was wasting all their time and should be working instead of going to school but she was determined to finish because she could make more as an LVN than she ever could working at the minimum wage jobs and would get paid for helping people.

The next day the phone rang and all she could hear was sobbing. "Hello?"

"I caught her in bed with my best friend. I thought she was the one. I loved her so much. I had left to go out to sea for a month and when I got home, she was in bed with my best friend. I hadn't told her that I was coming in. I had wanted to surprise her but I was the one that ended up getting surprised."

"Trey, I am so sorry. Are you ok?"

"No I am not. I just want to die. I am in California right now. They gave me a leave so that I could clear my head and I flew over to California to get away. I am staying with a buddy of mine that I was stationed with in Hawaii. I can't take this. I wish I would die, Hope. Life just isn't worth living when I am alone. I didn't just lose Danica but I also lost Jeremy. This is so unfair."

Her heart just dropped for him. They had not been married but a few months. "I am so sorry. I wish that I could take that pain from you. What did they say when they got busted? Trey, that stinks. Why don't you fly into Texas? Come spend time with your dad, mom, and me. You need to be around people who love you right now." She had tears welling up in her eyes and could not hold them back any longer. Why would that stupid girl do that? She would give anything in the world for Seth to treat her the way that Trey treated his wife. Every single time that he had called her, he had told her about the amazing things that he had done for his wife. Breakfast in bed all the time, roses all the time, just telling her over and over how much he loved her and needed her. She had heard him talk like that to her over the phone. It wasn't fair.

"They just told me that they were sorry and she told me that it was my fault for going out to sea. So it's my fault that she cheated on me when I was working to make money. Jeremy is also in the Navy and he is scheduled to go out to sea next month. Wonder how that will work out. She told me that she had fallen in love with him when I was gone. I just told them both that I wish them both the best and that I would be ok. I told her that I was happy for her because I didn't want her upset. I'm sorry but I just want to be alone. I can't come to Texas right now."

She thought seriously about how she wanted to jump into a plane and fly to California to be there for him so he didn't have to deal with this alone. Her husband would never let her though. "Trey, I am just a phone call away. Listen, I understand you are hurt and betrayed right now. Please do not hurt yourself. I can't stand the thought of something happening to you. If I had the money and Seth wasn't in the picture, I would fly to California to be there with you today. Please call me when you need to talk. I love you buddy." She could not help it but she was crying as hard as he was. Her heart was broken in two that he was having to deal with this.

"I promise I won't hurt myself. I just need time right now. Hope, you are truly the best friend that I have ever had. I am so lucky to have you. Seth is a lucky man. Talk to you later sweetheart. I love you and miss you."

"I love and miss you too and you are also my best friend." When Seth got home, he asked her why she was crying.

"Trey caught his wife and best friend in bed together. It just makes me sad for him. He called and was crying earlier. I am crying because I could not imagine how I would feel if I got betrayed by not only you but Mitzi as well."

"That poor guy. That sucks. I am sorry to hear that. I don't like him very much but I would not wish that on my worst enemy. Why did she cheat on him?"

"He had been out to sea and blamed him because he was out doing his job."

"That stupid witch knew that he was in the Navy when she married him. She knew that he would be leaving for long periods of time. Listen, right now he needs you. I support your friendship right now. I feel so sorry for him. He will need a good friend right now and honestly you are the best friend that anyone could ask for. Be there for him right now ok." Seth meant that about the friendship. Hope was the best friend that he had ever had. Her heart was huge and she would do anything for anyone. He really didn't know why he was so mean to her all the time.

"Ok, thanks for understanding." That was part of the reason she stayed. He could be very sweet at times. The next weeks were kind of a blur to her. Trey called her often to let her know what he was doing. He turned to alcohol and spent most of his time away from work getting drunk for awhile. He got transferred back to Hawaii and was happy about that because he didn't have to see them anymore. Days after he arrived in Hawaii, he got sent out to sea for 6 weeks.

When he was out, Hope sat down one day and got on her computer. She was checking her email when she noticed that yahoo messenger popped up. It was Seth's chat and a girl named Angie had written him. "Hey babe. Just wondering how you are doing. Hope we can get together again really soon. I had a great time with you last week." What was this? She looked at Angie's profile and the girl was from Abilene. Wait a second, she had seen several phone calls on their bill to Abilene and when she had asked Seth about them, he had told her that it was his boss. That had made sense since had had to drive to work in Abilene and people had to drive to work from all over. She went and got the phone bill and called the number on the bill.

"Hey babe. How have you been."

"Who are you and why have you been talking to my husband?"

"Excuse me. Who are you? Who is your husband?"

"Is this Angie? Seth is my husband. My name is Hope."

"Yea but you guys are separated. You have filed for divorce and ran off to Arlington with another man so why are you calling me to give me crap? You are the one that left him," Angie said hatefully.

"Um, wrong. I went to Arlington two weeks ago with my mom and dad to take mine and Seth's daughters to Six Flags. I did not run off to Arlington with a man. I went there with my parents. Yea my dad is a man but he is my dad."

"Daughters? Seth only has one daughter. Desirae. You must have your other daughter with another man."

"Wrong again sweetheart, we have Desirae and Kelsey. Desirae is 4 and Kelsey is 2. My parents went to Six Flags with me because their dad didn't want to go and my parents knew that it would be hard for me to keep up with both of them by myself. We went two Fridays ago."

"He has two kids? Why would he only tell me about one? I don't understand."

"Well, have you met him personally? Have you slept with him?"

"I just chat with him on messenger. I don't know him personally and why would I sleep with him?" Her voice wavered when she said that.

"Angie, wouldn't you want to know the truth if it was your husband? Please be honest with me."

"Oh man I am sorry. I lied to you Hope. I have met him and hung out with him at a restaurant and bar in Abilene. After that we did have a one night stand. He took me out and bought me a chicken fried steak dinner and then took me out for drinks. We drove back to Breckenridge to take his brother home with me following him. He dropped his brother off at his house and I met him at the hotel, where we had the one night stand. I understand now why his brother told him more than once at the bar that he was screwing up and would regret this. I thought he was being judgmental because y'all were not technically divorced yet and I am so sorry. I believed him when he told me that he would help me raise my daughter who has Downs Syndrome and I fell for his crap. I truly believed that he was not with you anymore. I am such an idiot. He told me that his mother was Pentecostal and that she didn't want me calling because he was living with her and thought it was wrong for him to even talk to another woman because the divorce was not final yet. It is hard for me to find a guy that will accept me because of the fact that my daughter's disabilities so I fell for him. I would never sleep with a married man on purpose. You have to believe me."

All at once, Hope felt the hot tears flowing out of her eyes. Could this be real? Seth was a jerk but had he really cheated on her? Angie heard her start to sob and felt like she was about 2 inches tall.

"I have a best friend who's daughter has Downs Syndrome. I would want to kill anyone who did that to her. That is so wrong. I am sorry he lied to you. I can't believe that he would be so sorry to pretend that he would raise your child who has Downs. I am sorry for what he did," she told her from the bottom of her heart. As much as she wanted to hate this woman, she couldn't. She pictured her friend Amelia falling for the same line one day and her heart went out to Angie.

Angie was shocked. Was this woman apologizing to her after she had been caught having an affair with that lady's husband? "Thanks. I guess he got us both. I am so sorry. I hope that you can forgive me one day. I truly would never do anything like this on purpose. I will send you emails to prove it to you. Plus you can use them in court. What is your email address? I will put an end to the affair tonight. The truth is if we had met under different circumstances, you and I would probably be friends.

"You are right. Thanks for the emails. I can use them in court. You can have him. I'm done. I have put up with years of mental abuse and this is the final straw. Maybe you and I can get together and do something one night. Maybe we can go have a drink together. You were both played by the same jerk so we can go make a toast to him. I can't believe this."

"I tell you what Hope, you let me know when you want to do it and I will buy you a drink or two. I owe at least that much to you after your husband bought my drinks and me food."

"Let's do it next week. I need to get out of here and cool off."

"Ok it's a plan." Angie got Hope's email address and they discussed when and where they would meet each other the next week. They said their goodbyes and got off the phone. Hope collapsed in the floor and bawled like a baby. She wept hard. She was torn. No matter what, she loved him just as much as the day she married him and could not picture her life without him but she decided that the infidelity was just one mistake too many. Through her tears, she went into their bedroom and packed every item of clothing that he had. When she was through with that, she picked her phone up and called his brother Troy. His girlfriend Shawna was the one that got the call.

"Hello."

She was screaming at Shawna when she told her what she needed to say. "You tell your piece of crap boyfriend of yours that I trusted him. I loved him just like a brother and I don't understand how he could betray me the way that he did. He was another brother to me. He has told me before that he loved me just like a sister and blood is not necessarily thicker than water. He is a lying jerk because when it came down to what was right, he backed up his brother who was in the wrong. Tell him that I hate him and that he has killed me just as much as Seth did. You tell him that he is as big a jerk as his brother and he ought to be ashamed for knowing and not telling me. Tell him that how dare him come into my house and pretend to be my friend knowing that his piece of crap brother had cheated on me. He just called me Sis yesterday. I hate him now and if you knew it, I hate you too. Goodbye!" Shawna could barely understand her through her tears and yelling. She knew right away that she was broken. It hurt Shawna to hear Hope so upset.

"Um I don't have any idea what you are talking about," she started to say just as the line went dead.

Troy had heard the screaming from the phone and he was on the other side of the room.

"What was that about Shawna?"

"Troy, you better tell me the truth. Did you know something about Seth cheating on Hope? That was Hope and she is very upset."

"Crap. Ok here goes nothing. You and I had split up. Well, Seth convinced me 2 weeks ago, when you and I were split up that he knew a nice girl that he wanted me to meet. I argued with him at first but finally went along with it and met her. Well, when we got to the restaurant there were two girls. I barely spoke to the girl that Seth wanted to set me up with but he seemed really interested in this girl named Angie. I had ridden to Abilene with him and the girls took their own cars. After the restaurant, everyone wanted to go to the club. I just wanted to go home. Well I was kind of at Seth's mercy since we had gone there in his car so we stayed out way too late but finally we went home. The girl that he wanted me to meet went home and I have not heard from her since then. I am sorry but we were split up at that time and I did not touch her. I noticed that Angie followed us to Breckenridge and I don't know how many times I told Seth that he was messing up and that he needed to stop doing what he was doing. If they slept together, I don't know about it, but I know that Angie's car followed us to Breckenridge. I don't know how many times I reminded him what he had at home and how he would throw it all away if he cheated. He kept promising me that he would not cheat and told me that they just wanted to hang out a little bit longer. I bet Hope hates me right now. I love her. She is as much of a sister to me as he is a brother. She is a great mama to those kids. I hate him right now. Not only did he throw his life away, he has managed to drag me into it also. I bet she will never forgive me."

"Troy just be honest with her like you were with me just now. Yes she is mad. I don't blame her but more than anything what I heard in her voice was hurt. She is hurt. She was just betrayed by her husband and you. I know that you are her brother in law but to her, you are a second brother so she is hurt. Don't be mad at her. That anger was caused by her hurt."

"I need to call mom and let her know what is going on. I would rather her hear it from me than to hear it from her. She is going to be so upset and hurt. She loves Hope too. Plus I have a feeling that she will be having my stupid brother living back with her for awhile now and she needs to know."

Hope had just finished pulling Seth's weight set out to the front porch with the bags that she had thrown out into the front yard. She had never been that mad. She was glad he was not home or he would probably have gotten hit. His weight set was very heavy and after yanking that thing outside, her back started to hurt a little so she said some loud cuss words. She heard a knock on the door and looked at the time. It was too early for the jerk to be home plus he would not have knocked. She opened the door to see her mother in law standing in front of her, looking broken. She loved her mother in law. "Hi," her mother in law said.

"Troy just called me so I came over to check on you. I am so sorry that my son did this to you and the kids. Please don't hate me."

"I could not hate you for what he did but I hate him right now."

"Baby, I want you to know that I love you just like a daughter. I have loved you like a daughter since I met you and this is killing me too. I am so sorry."

Her mother in law was crying which made her cry also. She reached out and hugged her mom in law, who held her close for a long time. "I don't want to lose my grandbabies."

"You won't have to. I would not even keep him from seeing the girls because they need all of you in their lives. I'm sorry that I have to make him leave. I can't do it anymore. I love you too. You have been good to me through the years. Please forgive me for never being good enough for him," she said sobbing. "I tried so hard but I never was good enough. I'm sorry for that." She broke down and told her mother in law a lot of what she had been going through for years. They were both crying.

"Sweetie, it was not you. You did the best you could. I would like to take him over my knee and spank him like he was a little boy but those days are over. What exactly happened? How did you find out?"

Hope sat down and started to tell her mother in law everything she knew at that point. When her mother in law went to leave, she picked up the bags of clothes out of the yard and loaded them in her car. "Can you let him know that he is welcome to come to our house and stay until he gets everything worked out? I don't approve of what he did but he is still my son."

"I will do that and I know."

That night when her husband got home, he asked why his workout bench and weights were on the front lawn. He saw his wife sitting alone in the living room crying.

"Because I found out about Angie. Don't deny it. She has sent me emails, the phone bill had her phone number on it, she confessed everything, then I called Troy and he told me what he knew. I hate you."

"What? Why would you think something like that? She must be lying. Why would my brother say something like that about me? He is lying, Hope."

"I tricked him and told him that you admitted it. Don't get mad at him. You are the only one to blame here. You cheated and got caught. Now get out. I am done."

"How can you throw our family away like this? How can you make me leave because of some girl that lied? She is a liar. I have never cheated. I should have since I got the blame anyway. She would have been a better lay than you anyway so I should have at least got my thrills since I got accused anyway."

"Seth shut-up," she screamed. "She sent me the emails. Quit lying. It is all there in black and white. Your own brother came out and admitted it because he thought I already knew. Stop lying. I have put up with your mental abuse, you controlling every single thing I ever did, your lies, you cussing me all the time, you breaking my stuff, and way too much crap over the years. I am done. The cheating was the final straw. I can't do it anymore. I am sorry. Your mom said that you could stay with her. I need you to leave. Now you can get the skinny girl that you want that will be a goddess in bed. You can get whatever pleases you all the time and I don't have to put up with your cussing me anymore. Get your butt out!"

Seth looked at her and walked past her into the kitchen and grabbed a knife and walked off. He walked out the door past her and she asked him why he needed a knife.

"Don't worry about it. I screwed up. I just threw our family away and I can't deal with it anymore. I have to go."

She felt a sense of panic. Was he going to attempt suicide? She was worried. She still loved him and did not want him to hurt himself. She did not realize it but that was a manipulation tactic that he was trying to use to get her to forgive him. He walked past her and ran down the road. She stayed in their front yard, calling his name. She could not leave her house. Her kids were sleeping but she didn't know what to do. Would he slit his wrists? He had threatened suicide before and who knows if he would really do it. She was scared. After he turned the corner down the street, she went back into her house and fell into the floor to her knees, crying and praying that he wouldn't hurt himself. She felt horrible. What if he killed himself? Would she ever be able to forgive herself? She felt like it would be her fault if he killed himself. She didn't know what to do. She considered calling the police and asking them to go look for him but if he didn't attempt it, he would be furious with her for calling them. After about an hour, he came back and knocked lightly on the door. She noticed the superficial scratches that he had made on his arms with the knife.

She answered, fearing that it may be the cops coming to tell her that his body had been found. It was Seth. "I'm sorry. I have done you and our daughters wrong for years. Can you please forgive me?" He was crying.

"Seth, please make this easy on both of us. Please go stay with your mom. I can't live with you anymore. I can't keep putting up with this. I am sorry. I will always love you but I can't do this anymore. I am done. Please leave. No I don't forgive you."

"What about the girls? They are going to need their daddy."

"Seth, they didn't have their daddy by their side when he was sleeping around. You have barely been there for them at all their entire life. Why do you think that I would believe that you would be there for them now? You have never changed their diaper or gotten up with them in the middle of the night. You can be their daddy from a different house. I am sorry. I just can't go on like this."

"Hope, please. Please don't make me leave."

"Seth please go. I need to be alone."

"Can I please go look at the girls and give them kisses Hope?"

"Yes. While you are doing that, I want to just go take a walk. I need to get away from you. Stay here until I get back then you need to go to your mom's house." She took off walking, despite the fact that it was after 2AM. She just needed time to think. She walked for about five miles, looking into the doors of her nursing school, thinking that she would have to quit the next day since she no longer had a husband to help her financially since they were going to be getting a divorce soon. Her heart felt like it was made of lead. She had passed two semesters and was going to have to quit on her third and final semester. This seemed so unfair. She knew that if she withdrew from the program that she would have to start completely over if she ever decided to go back. She walked to a church that was right down the street from her house and tried to go inside, thinking that the doors may possibly be open for her to go inside to use the alter. She seriously doubted that it would be open but it was a church so maybe they kept their doors open all the time. No such luck. She said a prayer and then started walking home. About that time, she felt a raindrop hit her on the arm and she suddenly was in the middle of a downpour. She could not help but feel like this was God's way of telling her that he was against her on this. She had made the promise for better or worse but now that the worst was here, she was walking away. She felt like even God had turned on her. She went back home and Seth was sitting on the couch.

"Can we please talk about this? I really want to work this out. Please. I know that I was wrong. I can't lose you and my babies. You all are my everything. Please Hope. I am sorry."

"No, you did plenty of talking to Angie. Please leave."

"Hope, please."

"Seth, I am done. I can't do this anymore. I am sick of the mental abuse and the name calling anyway. I am sick and tired of you hurting me. I am done this time for good." He left the house and walked to his mother's house since the only car they had was the one that her parents had given to her for graduation. She went to sleep but sleep did not come easily. The next day she got a call from her mom that 2 planes had just been flown into the World Trade Center in New York. Later that morning another plane hit the Pentagon and went down in a field because of terrorist attacks. Here she was fixing to go through a divorce and then found out that America was going to war less than 24 hours later. She could not help but worry about what would happen to Trey. Since he was Navy, there was a good possibility that he would end up at war. Life was so unfair. She could possibly lose her husband and her best friend soon. She wept for America and for herself. She would never forget how she felt in that 24 hour period. Her mom called her back about an hour later and asked her why Seth was staying with his mother. That was one thing she hated about living in such a small town. Everyone knew your business way too quickly. She explained to her mom that she had found out that Seth had cheated on her. Her mom was really sorry to hear that. Seth was really mean to her daughter but she still hated that they were not going to be able to work things out because they did have babies together. She opened up to her mom at that point how bad he had truly been to her over the years. She did not tell her everything though. She didn't think that she ever would open up that much.

"Why didn't you tell me before?"

"Because I was not ready to face this. Mom, I can't keep taking everything that he has done to me. I am done."

"I don't blame you. You put up with him years more than I would have. We saw how mean he was to you but we didn't see exactly how bad it was until you just told me."

"It just stinks Mom because I love him. Now the girls are going to have to live in a home with only a mama. I am not sure that I can do this."

"Baby, it may be easier to live in that house without him there to bring you down. I think that you are going to be happier now once you get past the initial shock."

"Maybe. Mom, I did not sleep much at all last night, can I please get off the phone and just go rest for a bit? He came by and got the girls and took them with him for a bit today. His mama wanted to see them also."

"Are you sure that is a good idea? What if he leaves with them?"

"He won't." She knew that he loved his daughters but that he would never run off with them because he would have to take care of them without anyone to help him and he could not do that.

"Ok, get you some rest. If you need us, we are here for you."

"I know that mom."

She slept like a baby until the phone rang. She got up and answered it, kind of hoping that it was Seth calling to beg for forgiveness because she could not help but still love him but instead it was Trey. "Hey Goober, what's up? How is life treating you?" When she heard his voice, she broke and started crying into the phone. At first he could not hear anything that she was saying because she was weeping so hard.

"He is gone. He was cheating and I made him leave." For the first time ever, she broke down and confessed all the mental abuse she had put up with for years. She cried and told him how he once locked her in her own house, where she could not get to her babies because he wanted to punish her, how he had disconnected the cables to her car so that she could not leave once, and all the stuff that she had put up with over the years. She told him that he had even hit her before but that she thought it was her own fault. If only she had not stood up for herself that day, he would not have hit her. She admitted stuff to him that she did not even tell his mom or hers. She was not sure why she was confessing everything to him the way that she was but she poured it all out. "I'm sorry, how are you doing without Danica? I'm so selfish right now. Plus America had been attacked and you are probably going to have to go off to war," she said sobbing.

"Hope, I'm ok. Going to stay with my buddy for those few weeks was exactly what I needed. We were not even together for long anyway. I thought that I would never get over her but I will be fine. If I go to war, I will do whatever I have to do to get home. It's my job. I don't want to go to war, but if I have to, I will do it for my country and for you and your kids. I will be fighting for my mom and dad and the things that really matter to me. If it takes me having to give my life, I don't want to but I would give it for my country if I have to. If I have to give my life, I will die a hero."

"Please don't talk about that Trey. I don't want to lose you too. I just got you back in my life and right now I don't think I will be able to make it without you. He is all I've ever known but you have always been my best friend. I need you."

"Yea I know and there are much better guys out there than him. There are guys that would never call you names. There are guys that believe that you are the center of their world. They know that your kids are a wonderful bonuses to an already great package. Most guys don't hit women Hope. Guys like me still exist," he told her.

"Yea and I thank God for guys like you. It is so unfair. Danica had such a wonderful guy and she threw him away. I was a good wife and mom and my husband threw me away. I don't understand. You help to remind me that nice guys are still around." They talked for a couple hours until he told her that his phone card was about to run out.

"I am so sorry. I forget that you do not have a phone over there. Thanks for listening to me."

"Any guy that would not listen to you would be crazy. Hey, I will call you tomorrow ok. I'm here for you, beautiful." At that point, the phone went dead. She was surprised that he had called her beautiful. He never talked to her like that. She placed the phone back on the charger and somehow felt a little better about her life, kind of like things would be better somehow. She got out of bed and got dressed. That day, her husband came by and brought her favorite food, southern syle codfish to her that he had gone and bought for her from Kens. Kens was a local restaurant that she loved.

"Thank you."

"You are welcome. Can I ask a big favor of you? Is there anyway possible that you can please take me to work tomorrow? I have a ride for today but there is no way I have one for tomorrow and if I don't have a ride, I will lose my job."

"You work an hour away."

"I know and I can get someone to bring me home but I can't get a ride up there. I am sorry."

"Fine. I will do it once."

"Great, I will give you some money for gas. I get paid tomorrow. Why didn't you go to school?"

"Don't feel like it."

"Oh, I understand. You do realize that since you won't let me come home that you are going to have to find a way to support yourself and you can't do that and be in school. I don't have enough money to support my place and your place so you are going to have to work or you and the kids will have to starve and lose the house. That's just how it works. I have a great idea. How about we become roommates? I will move to the girls bedroom and you can keep our room. I will stay here and pay the bills to help you get out of nursing school and you can do what you want to do and I will do what I want to do."

"What do you mean that you will do what you want to do and I can do what I want to do?"

"Well, if I want to go on a date and bring her home later after the date, I will. You can do the same thing. That way we are just roommates. Plus if something happens to happen between you and I then that is a bonus. We can be roommates with benefits if you would like to. You can finish school and you and the kids won't starve. If I don't stay here, you and I both know that you will never make it. You will never find someone that loves you anyway. You have two kids and having kids has screwed up your body really bad anyway. Nobody would want you anymore anyway."

"Well, that sounds like that would really help me out, now don't it. You sit here telling me that I could bring someone home if I wanted but then turn around and tell me that nobody would want me anyway. No thanks. You can keep living with your mom. My kids and I will never starve because my parents would never allow us to starve. I will take care of me and my kids. I will take you to court and they will make you pay child support. That is not too much to ask. I would rather be alone and struggle than to have you bring some girl home with you and have to see that crap. You seriously think I would be your roommate with benefits? You think that I would make love to you when you are bringing other women home? How dare you even think of me like that. You were my first kiss, love, and I gave my virginity to you. I don't know anyone else in that way and don't ever want to."

"Well if you make me move, I won't be able to give child support. The roommate with benefits idea is a great idea. That away if you wanted to get to know Trey better when he comes home on leave, you can. He would love that and you could get that out of your system. You know you want him."

"Trey and I are just friends Jerk. You make decent money. You will be able to give your kids some of it. You should want to do that for them."

"Well you will have to take me to court because I don't plan on giving it willingly. I just can not help you and also get a place for myself so why don't you just let me stay here and stay in a different room? I'm doing this for you."

"You want to do this for yourself, Seth. Don't play those mind games with me. If you were so interested in your family, you would not have been out cheating but thanks for the food." She was hungry so she was glad that he had gotten that for her. She knew him very well and knew that he was just trying to work his way back in.

"Do you not love me anymore Hope?"

"I will always love you, Seth. You gave me the most wonderful gifts I will ever have. You gave me Desirae and Kelsey. I got the best of you when you gave me them. I will always love you because you gave me wonderful daughters. I will always love you because you were my first love and I love who you could be. I don't love the way that you have treated me over the past several years so I'm done."

"Fine, you can quit nursing school or you and the kids can starve then. I don't care. You are the one making this choice Hope." At that point, he started calling her all the cuss words that she had grown accustomed to over the years.

"I will do what has to be done in order to survive."

"Fine go become a hooker then. The way you flaunt yourself at Trey, you might as well be one."

He then left and slammed the door behind him, knocking a picture off the wall. This was going to be so hard but she could do it. At least she would not have to deal with that kind of stuff anymore.

She ate a little bit of the food then put the rest in the icebox for later. After that, she gathered the last bit of strength left in her and drove to the college to quit nursing school. Her teachers tried to talk her out of quitting but she explained that she had to work. She did not think that she would ever make it financially without a job. By the end of the day, she had landed a full time job at a department store and started working at a local bar where she would waitress on weekends. This may be the worse pain she ever felt but she was determined not to allow it to break her. At that time, she did not realize how big of a blessing that this would be in the long run. She tried to take him back and give him another chance once after that just to get hurt really bad again when he went to a bar-b-q with another woman and lied that he was with his brother when he wasn't. This time when he did that, his brother Troy would not lie for him and told her the truth when she called and asked for Seth.

Troy forgave her for yelling at Shawna that night and came over and apologized to her for not telling her. He explained that she would always be a sister to him and that he loved her very much but that Seth had left him in a really awkward situation. He asked for forgiveness and she gave it. They would remain close for the rest of their lives.

When he got home that night, the crap hit the fan again and she told him to get out now and not come back. She was done and this time it was for good. She had given it a second chance only to be hurt again. Trey called right in the middle of their fight and Seth was the one that answered the phone. When he heard Trey's voice, he told him, "I am glad you called. Maybe you can calm her down. I messed up again and she is crying and is yelling at me. Maybe you can make her not so upset. I can't do anything right." He said that to make her look bad to Trey because he didn't want him to want her. It was another manipulation technique that he figured he would use. Trey did not buy it though.

"Just put her on the phone for me please."

"You got it." Seth looked at Hope and told her that it was Trey and that he was going to go home now. She got on the phone again crying. Trey once again had her smiling by the time that he got off the phone.

# Chapter 3

## The Surprise

The days went by and things started to get a little easier for Hope. Seth didn't stay with his mom but a couple weeks until he moved in with a lady that he worked with named Tanesha. At first it was very awkward for Hope and Seth to be friends and there was some major hurt feelings and anger between them. Trey made it a point to call her every single day when he was not out at sea. He had become the rock that had kept her from drowning as she went through the divorce and the hurt feelings. She would write him almost everyday whatever she was feeling. He was the best friend that she had ever had and somehow just telling him about how she felt made her feel better. Hearing his voice made her happy. Somehow just from talking on the phone and writing him, she had started to feel something for him that she had never felt before. She had started to have feelings for him and was beginning to realize that she was falling in love with him.

At one point, she wrote in the letter to him that she kind of wished that he lived closer and that she could imagine herself becoming his girlfriend. She also told him that she could easily think of him as more than just a friend. She mailed it that night because she knew that she would chicken out if she didn't mail it quickly. About two weeks after she mailed it, she couldn't believe that she had told him that and suddenly got embarrassed by it. He called her that night and asked how his girls were. "We are good. How are you? How is work?"

"We are all good here. I am very homesick though. I wish that I could come home really bad."

"I wish you could come home too. I miss you."

"I miss you too Hope. Have you heard anything about the divorce?"

"The papers have been filed and I am just waiting for the time when I can get it all over with. Hey Trey, I have to ask you a favor. I wrote a letter on January 25 and I need you to promise me that when you get it, you will not read it. Please."

"I read all my letters. Your letters are a big part of what keeps me going. Why would I not read one of your letters? Tell me what is so important in that letter for you to not want me to read it."

"Don't worry about what is in it. Just please promise me that you will not read it. Tear it up when you get it please."

"I can't do that. I will make you that promise if you tell me now what was in it but otherwise I can't make you that promise. I want to know what is in it more than anything right now for you to want me to throw it away. Just tell me."

"Look, it is something that I should have never said. I don't want you to read it. It is embarrassing."

"Just tell me. Tell me or I am gonna quit calling you until after I read it."

"Ok, I just told you something stupid about myself and something dumb I did in high school."

"No you didn't. Don't lie. I can tell in your voice that you are telling me that just so that I will quit asking you about it. Just say it and it will be over with."

"Gosh darnitt, I told you that I wish you lived closer and that I could see you being my boyfriend if you lived closer. Somehow my feelings have grown into something more. I know they should not have though so please forget what I said. Ok. I know it is stupid and I am sorry."

"Ok, now was that so bad? Was that so hard? I could see myself as something more to you also. I have had liked you ever since I was in the eighth grade."

That statement took her breath away for a minute. Wow. He had those same feelings that she was having since eighth grade.

"Since eighth grade? Too bad you live in Hawaii. If you lived in Galveston or Corpus, you would not be quiet so far away."

"I know. I wish I lived closer. I have put in a transfer for Texas. Days like today I hate the Navy. I want to be there with you and the girls."

Wow, he could be so sweet. Why had she wasted so many years on Seth when this wonderful guy had liked her this entire time? It would not be fair to him though. She had two babies and he didn't have any. "Seth was an idiot for letting you go. He is missing out on a wonderful person with some amazing little bonuses. Guess what, I'm supposed to get a leave from work in about three months. I plan on coming home and spending a lot of time with you and the girls when I get there. I miss you and I want to get to know the girls better."

"Wow, you will have to let me know. I can take off work and come get you from the airport. I can't wait."

"I may stay with you some when I come down if that is ok. I know you have a floor or a couch I could use. I want to spend all the time that I can with you when I come down."

"Of course. You are always welcome here. My house is your house but I would never make you sleep on the floor. I'm sure we could find a place in the dog house or outside on a blanket for you. I guess you can maybe take the couch too," she said, teasing him.

"If I sleep in the doghouse then your dog would not have a place to sleep."

She started to giggle and let him know that the dog usually sleeps with her.

"Well, you could stick me out on your lawn, under the stars. That would be way better than a submarine, bunked up with a hundred other men passing gas or even better I could steal the dog's spot."

She blushed about the dogs spot comment. "Bless your heart. I think anything would be better than that. Also in a sub there is no place to run. I'm not sure that you would want to steal the dog's spot."

"I'd love to steal the dog's spot. That's no lie about the sub. Well, I am looking forward to seeing you but that isn't for three months so we will just have to make some plans for when I come to town. I can't wait."

"Sounds great."

"Hey beautiful, I need to get off here. I am exhausted and I have to be up really early in the morning for something at work. I miss you and truly can't wait to see you."

"I know, Freshman, three months will be here before we know it. I will mark it on my calendar and be waiting."

"Will you ever quit calling me freshman and let me grow up to be a sophomore? I think that I should qualify as a sophomore by now." Freshman was a nickname that she had given to him when he was a freshman in high school and throughout the years, it had stuck in her click of friends.

"Probably not," she told him.

"I kind of figured. Good night."

The next day, she went to work like she always did but after her lunch, a coworker came up to her and asked her if her friend had ever found her.

"Who are you talking about?"

"I'm talking about the McDaniel boy. He was here, asking for you. I told him that you were working in the pharmacy." She stopped walking and looked at him like he was crazy.

"What are you talking about? The only McDaniel friend that I have is in Hawaii. Was it his step-brother or his father?"

"I think his name is Trey or Trace or something like that."

"No, he isn't here. He is in Hawaii. I just talked to him last night and he was in Hawaii," she said very confused.

"No sweetheart, I sent him to the pharmacy to look for you about five minutes ago." She had been working in the pharmacy stocking for them.

"No way. That's not possible. For real? I gotta go out there. If it is Trey, he just got back from Hawaii. We just talked on the phone last night and he did not tell me he was coming but he is good at surprises."

"Yea, it is the one that is in the Navy. He said that he was here for awhile on a short leave. Sorry I did not know that it was a surprise."

She said thanks then almost ran to the pharmacy, scanning the store all the way there. She could feel the excitement building up inside of her. Why would he come all the way here and not bother to tell her? She looked around and did not see him anywhere. She started looking further. When she got to the pharmacy a coworker told her that some guy had been there looking for her and they told him that she would be back in about 10 minutes. Was it true? Had he really came home from Hawaii? "Who was the guy?'

"I'm not sure but he was cute. He had brown hair and pretty green eyes. He said that he will be back. He is cuter than Seth. I never liked Seth. Plus he looked really good in a military uniform."

"If it is who I think it is then it is my best friend. Can I run look through the store really quick? I will be really fast."

"Sure, just hurry before the pharmacist gets back from lunch."

"Ok great, thanks." She ran and did a quick scan of the entire store and did not find him so she went to work. She had decided that it must be someone else when she heard the familiar voice behind her.

"Hey goober." She jumped up from her squatting position and threw her arms around him and cried into his shoulder. They were happy tears though, not sad tears.

"Why didn't you tell me you were coming?"

"Surprise! I wanted to surprise you."

"Well, I would have taken off work to spend time with you if I had known. God I have missed you so much."

"I've missed you too." They were still hugging when he picked her up and twirled her around. "Nope, it is worth it to see this surprised look on your face and these happy tears to not tell you. I may not get to see you as long as I would if I had told you but I get the amazing memory of seeing this surprised look on your face."

"I get off at 6. Can you come by my house then?"

"I will be there at 6:15 to give you time to get home. I want to spend as much time with you as I can."

"I still can't believe you are here." She could feel the warm tears streaming down her cheeks and did not even care. He reached up and wiped them from her cheeks and kissed her lightly on her forehead.

"I will have to drive to Houston and see my mom and go to my Uncle's funeral. He passed away so they approved me to have a weeks leave. I hate it that I had to come in for that but I am so glad to get to see you."

"I'm sorry about your uncle."

"Me too. See you at 6:15 or 6:30."

"Hey, I am going to a concert on Friday. If you are back, you want to go with me?"

"I will be back and yes of course I would love it."

"Ok, see you tonight. He quit hugging her and walked off then turned around and hugged her again. "I'm sorry but I just missed you so much. It is so good to see you. I deserve another hug after flying in from Hawaii to see you," he said and smiled. As she hugged him a second time, she felt another couple tears sliding down her face. He pulled away and kissed the top of her head again then walked off.

"Woohoo. I'm going to call Della and tell her that you have a stud muffin you have not told us about," her coworker Dena told her. Dena and Della had been best friends for years.

"Della already knows about Trey. She used to be mean to him in high school when he would call for me because she was waiting on her boyfriend to call. She knows that he has been my friend for years."

"Um hum she never seen your friend pick you up and show a display of affection like that, has she? Friend my butt. That man is after a little something more than friendship. He likes you and you cried when you saw him so I know that you like him as more than a friend. I am sorry but this guy is way cuter than Seth. Plus that uniform. If you don't want him, I will take him in a heartbeat."

"Hm, maybe you might ought to call and tell Della on me cause I do like him a lot. She don't know it yet but I invited him to go to watch the Lonestar concert with us Friday night so you are going to have to find your own military man," she said grinning.

"Well, I think that he is cute."

"Do you think they will let me off about 20 minutes early tonight? I got to rush home and clean up my house before he gets there."

"Yea, I think that can be arranged. Why don't you go home at 5 and I will stay until 6 for you?"

"Really?"

"Yea, that will give you more time."

"Thanks Dena."

"I don't know why you have to go clean your house. You keep it spotless."

"I just need to pick it up. I do have little ones and they may have left toys out and stuff."

"Ok if you don't start seeing this guy I'm really going to steal him from you. You really should have just skipped Seth and went for this guy. Plus he is a Navy guy and we all know how good they look in their uniforms. This guy rocked that uniform."

She just smiled at Dena then went back to work. Her shift seemed like it drug by because she wanted to be with him so badly. As soon as she got off, she was trying to rush out the door and Sarah stopped her on the way out. Sarah was her friend Amelia's mom. "Was that guy you were hugging on Trey?"

"Yes, he came home from Hawaii and surprised me."

"That's cool. I knew it had to be him because I saw y'all hugging and when you finally came up for air, he grabbed you up and hugged you again." Hope smiled.

"He's coming over at 6:15 so I got to hurry home. I've got to clean the house really quick before he gets there and then I gotta go grab the girls from mom's house."

"Ok but your house is clean all the time."

"I just want it to be spotless ok."

"Oh ok. You kids have fun."

"We will."

"Oh and by the way, he is cuter than I remember him."

"I know," she said and winked at Sarah. Sarah grinned. She hoped that something would happen and Hope could end up with Trey. She had really been hurt by Seth and seemed happy for the first time in a long time.

Hope sped home and within minutes she had the toilet scrubbed, floors swept and mopped and was starting to dust. She then threw on some cuter clothes and then Della called her.

"Hey, you want to come eat with me tonight? I want to take the kids all out to eat." Della had a daughter that was one month older than Desirae named Alex.

"No, I'm about to have company."

"Who?"

"Trey came in from Hawaii. I would like the kids to be home so he can see them."

"Well, I'm going to take them out to eat first. Trey is here? Wow. I thought he was in the Army or something."

"Navy and he flew in today because his uncle passed away so he has to go to Houston and he is going to come see me tonight."

"Well, I am going to take the girls to eat and I will bring them home when I get back. You better not do anything I would do," she said laughing.

"Well, don't keep the girls too long. He wants to see them."

"Ok, I will have them home soon. Have a good time."

"We will. Gotta go, he is knocking. Bye."

She answered the door and he pulled her close to him again and hugged her. "Hey, I've missed you since I seen you at work."

"How was your day?"

"Great, I went and spent some time with dad while you were working. He took me to a late lunch earlier. You hungry? I can take you to get something."

"Oh no, I am still full from lunch. Where's my girls?"

"Della has them. She wanted to take them out to eat. We will have to go get them when they are done."

"Awesome. I am looking forward to seeing them. So, how have you been?"

"As crazy as this sounds, much better. It feels like life has started over but it is getting better everyday."

"That's great. I think that things will keep getting better everyday instead of worse. Do you still love him?"

"You know a part of me will always love him because he gave me Desirae and Kelsey. I got the best part of him with them but no I don't think I am in love with him anymore. You want to hear something funny? He told a friend of mine that we split up because I had an affair with you when you were in Guam."

"Wow, I nailed you from Guam? I must be very talented." They both laughed. Hey, do you have any of your yearbooks from school?"

"Yea, of course." She ran to her closet and grabbed her yearbooks and handed them to him when they started to reminisce about when they were in high school. They discussed the past, each other, and funny memories until the door floor open and Desirae and Alex ran in. Della came in behind her carrying Kelsey.

"We enjoyed ourselves. Here is a burrito. Desirae said that we needed to get her mommy something too. Plus I know you didn't eat anything yet."

"Thanks. Let me get you some money Della."

"Nah don't worry about it. It's my treat tonight. You can pay next time."

"Hi Trey, this is Alex and this is Della."

"I have known Della a long time. She used to be mean to me in high school when I would call your mama." Della started to laugh. "It's because I was afraid my boyfriend at the time would call when you were tying up the phone. He was army, you know. I had to talk when he was available."

"She was mean to all my friends, not just you."

"I understand that now that I am also in the military. We don't get a lot of time to call people."

"Hey can I get you to go grab the car seat?"

"Of course," Hope said, getting up and heading toward the door.

"I can get it. Want me to put it in your car? Just because I don't have kids don't mean that I can't figure out how to operate a car seat," Trey said. "I ran into Amelia earlier today and she told me that she wanted us to come by her house anyway so let's run over there and see her. I would love to spend a little time with her."

"Sounds good. I need to catch up with Amelia and Sarah anyway." Della and Alex said their goodbyes and left in their car while Trey tried to install the car seat. Hope stood back and smiled as he struggled to install it then get Kelsey buckled in.

"It was a little harder than I thought it would be," he admitted.

"Yea they are not easy at all."

"That's ok. She's worth it. Your kids are amazing. They are beautiful and wonderful just like their mama."

She felt the color coming to her cheeks and felt herself blushing a little bit. "Thank you Trey."

He smiled at her. She drove them to Amelia's house where they all got out and went inside and caught up on old times. She could not help but notice how well he got along with her girls. They loved playing with him. He was so good with them. She had not seen Seth play with them like that in a long time. She liked it a lot. Listening to their laughter made her laugh as well. Amelia gave her a knowing look. Hope had not come out and told her but she knew that Hope had fallen for him since her husband had left. She could tell just by watching them. The feelings were there and were very strong. They left after about an hour and went back to Hope's house where he played with the girls until she told them that it was time for them to go to bed. "Awe mama," Desirae said yawning.

"It is getting late and Trey and I want to keep talking for a little bit before he has to go home."

"I will tell you what. Your mama will let y'all sleep with her if you both give me a big hug goodnight. I love you girls." Desirae and Kelsey both gave their mama and Trey a big hug then Desirae asked her mama to come tuck them in. She reminded her that it was story time.

"I may be a minute, would you like to watch a movie or listen to music for a bit?"

"Yea, a movie sounds great," he told her. She handed him the remote to the tv and showed him where the vcr tapes were. He picked out Armageddon then put it into the vcr and pushed play. She left the room to tuck her babies into bed and tell them a quick story. By the time the story was over, both kids were sound asleep. She came back out and seen him sitting on the couch watching tv so she sat down next to him. "You want to hear a confession?"

"Yea," she answered.

"I had already read that letter that you were so concerned about me reading that night you asked me about it but I didn't want to tell you because I wanted to hear you tell me."

"That's not nice. I had to be embarrassed twice because of that. Thanks a lot. Let's not talk about it. I'm embarrassed about that stupid letter."

"You want to hear something? You have had something truly special to me for a long time. You have had a piece of my heart ever since you let my balloon go when I was in the seventh grade. You may have let my balloon go but you never let my heart go."

"You have really had a crush on me for that long?" "It isn't a crush. You are my best friend. You are beautiful. You are special to me. I can't explain it but I feel like I am the luckiest guy in the world right now because I am here with you."

"I feel like the luckiest girl in the world too. You are my best friend and you got me through the hardest time of my life. You love my kids. How could I ever ask for more than that?"

"You know, there is something that I have wanted to do for the past 10 years and I never had the opportunity to do it. I have wanted to do it since the first time I ever met you."

She swallowed and asked what he wanted to do. "Kiss you. You can stop me if you want to."

He leaned in and kissed her softly on her lips. She felt a quiver go up her down her spine.

"Should I stop?"

"No," she told him. He kissed her deeply and put his arms around her. In that moment, she felt every single emotion humanly possible. Excitement from his lips on hers and his tongue softly caressing hers. Pure love for him that she could not explain. She felt a little guilty because she was still technically married, felt happiness for being right where she was right then, terror because she knew that he would have to go back to Hawaii and would have to leave her again. She could not bare the thought of him leaving her again. Her heart was pounding as he laid down with her and they made out right there on her couch. She was so excited. She had not ever felt this kind of emotions for Seth that she was feeling right at that moment, wrapped in his arms. When he broke for air, he held her very tightly to him.

"Wow that kiss was worth waiting ten years for," he told her. He held her close to him. Let's turn this movie off and listen to some music. There was a song that I heard just before I got on the plane and it made me think of you. I'm hoping they play it."

"What is the name of the song?"

"Good morning beautiful. I was thinking that I would get to see you and hopefully wake up close to you, even if it is with me down the hall from you. I know that the dog needs her spot in bed with you," he said, teasing her. "I mean I already slept with you when I was living in Guam so I'm sure that being down the hall from you and seeing your beautiful face would be just as awesome."

"That's a beautiful song. I have heard it. Yea, you are talented to nail me from Guam. The song that reminds me of you is I'm already there by Lonestar," she told him. They both were smiling. She reached to the coffee table and grabbed the remote for the stereo and then turned off the tv. He pulled her close to him again and held her tightly in his arms, snuggling into her.

"Did you ever think that we would ever be where we are at right now in high school?" she asked him, barely breathing.

"Nope, I thought that Seth would have you for the rest of your life. I had given up on ever touching you like this. Maybe we can sleep together tonight. I am not talking about sex but just waking up together, in each other's arms. I would really like that. We can lay right here on the couch like we are right now. I just want to feel you near me."

"Me too Trey." As if it were meant to be, the radio DJ announced that the next song he was going to play was Good Morning Beautiful.

"Come on, get up. I want to dance with you," he told her, jumping to his feet. He took her by the hand and pulled her to her feet where he placed his forehead on hers and started to dance very slowly while looking in her eyes. As they were dancing, he would sing the part of the song that he knew. She could feel the tears welling up in her eyes. Seth had never treated her this good. She could tell by the way that Trey was looking at her that he truly loved her. She put her head on his shoulder and listened to him singing to her. This was one of the most memorable moments that she would ever have in her entire lifetime. The sound of his sweet voice singing to her, the feel of his warm strong arms around her, the smell of his scent would forever live with her. For the first time in her entire life, she felt what it was like to have a guy that truly cared for her. It felt awesome. As they were dancing, it was more like they were barely moving their feet. They were lost in their own world together as they danced. When the song ended, he started to yawn.

"What time do you need to leave for Houston?"

"About 4AM."

"What? Trey, it is almost 1AM. You are going to be so sleepy."

"Ok you are right. I don't really care. I don't want to miss a single minute with you."

"Ok, how about this then? I will lay down with you and we can sleep together? That away you don't have to miss any time with me. You can hold me as we sleep."

He grinned at her. "Do you think I will really be able to keep my hands off you if you are sleeping next to me?"

She grinned really big. "Come on, let's get some sleep. I don't want you to wreck on the way to Houston tomorrow. That would kill me." She took him by the hand and led him to the bedroom her daughters shared. "I'm sorry but the bed is kind of small."

"Good, that gives us more of an opportunity to be even closer to each other in the bed."

They laid down on the bed. He looked into her eyes and took her by the hand. They laid there for a long time, just staring at each other and he leaned over and started to kiss her again. Before they knew it, they had made out for 3 hours straight. He kept his word to her and never tried to get her to have sex with him that night. He wanted to and she wanted it just as bad but he was a total gentleman about it. When his watch beeped, he groaned.

"I don't want to leave."

"I don't want you to leave either. Wish I could go with you to support you in your uncles death."

"Me too beautiful. This has been the greatest night of my life."

"I know exactly what you mean. It has been the best night of mine also. Gosh, you are going to be so sleepy today when you are driving. I'm sorry."

"You are worth it. I will be careful. You are sorry for giving me the greatest night of my life?"

She smiled. "You hungry? I can make you some breakfast."

"Oh no, I'm not hungry and I gotta get on the road. I'm sorry I have to leave but I will be back for the concert. I can't wait to see you again. It is going to be so hard to go back to Hawaii."

"Me too. I will be counting the hours. I am so glad that you surprised me. I hate it about your uncle but I am so happy that you surprised me."

"Yea well you surprised me when you didn't make me stop kissing you. My life is so much better after today happened."

She answered him with the biggest smile that he ever seen spread across her face.

"You know, Seth was an idiot for letting you go. He was the luckiest guy on earth and he let it go. I don't understand. You are beautiful."

"That's how I feel about Danica but I am thankful that she let you go because I got you out of her stupidity."

"I am so happy. I will see you in a couple days."

"Ok, I can't wait."

He went to the restroom then kissed her goodbye. She heard his car start then he walked back in the door. "I'm sorry. I had one more thing to say. He then began to sing. "Good morning beautiful how was your night? Mine was wonderful with you by my side. When I opened my eyes and saw your sweet face, it's a good morning beautiful day. Have a great couple days beautiful."

She leaned into him and kissed him this time. He walked out the door and headed out for Houston. She knew that he had a long, hard drive ahead of him and hoped that he made it there safe after she kept him up all night. She turned all the lights off and crawled into bed with her children. She could not believe that night had just happened.

Desirae was up a few hours later and Seth was supposed to come by and pick up the girls to take them to his house for the day. She fed both kids then got them ready to go see their dad. After they ate, he showed up to get them and she hugged and kissed them both.

"What's up with you? Why are you smiling like that?"

"I didn't realize I was smiling," she told Seth.

"You are grinning from ear to ear. It's kind of sickening. If I didn't know any better, I'd think you had just been laid."

"Nope," she told him truthfully.

"Ok, well you have a good day. I will take good care of them."

"I know," she told him. He put both kids in the car and about an hour later, her phone rang.

"What the hell is going on? What is this about Trey coming to see you? Desirae told me that he was there when she went to bed last night. What's his problem? I'm ready to kill him."

"He don't have a problem. He is doing perfectly well."

"Why is he here? Some stupid leave?"

"Nope, he came in cause his uncle passed away and he surprised me."

"That jerk is full of surprises. This is bullcrap. He has no business being at my house with my kids and my wife. You tell him that the war has started and he better get his army butt back to Hawaii."

"For starters, it is not your house anymore and I am not your wife anymore. Secondly, I can take the kids around anyone that I want to and he isn't a bad guy so I don't see what your problem is there. You allowed him to come over before when we were together so why are you so concerned about it now? The kids are not in any danger with him so you don't have any say so about that. Also you are living with another woman, so you don't have any say so about who comes and stays late at my house. We are getting divorced. The papers have been filed and we are just waiting on the lawyers at this point. Plus you know that he is in the Navy, not the Army so don't be stupid."

"You are still my wife. We are not divorced yet. It isn't right. It isn't right that you let another guy come over there and stay all hours of the night. You have no right. Look, this is not cool. You are my wife. It isn't the same. When I see her standing there, she is not you. I miss you. We need to do what we can to work this out. I want to come home. I am ready to be the husband that I should have been years ago. I have learned my lesson. Please. It isn't the same. I know that you have had sex with him and it will be hard to forget that but I am willing to try. Please let me come home."

"You are right, Seth. It is not the same. I don't want to get back with you. A part of me will always love you but I am not in love with you anymore. I'm ready to move on with my life. I am sick of the mental abuse. I am sick of the cheating and the crap. I am done."

"You mean you are ready to move on with that home wrecking jerk? This is all his fault. If he hadn't come over, we would be fine. I hate him. He deserves to have his butt whipped. He better not be there when I come back to bring the girls back. I will kick his butt. He will think that he entered World War 3."

"Yea Seth, we would be perfectly fine if he hadn't come to see me. I would still be alone and you would still be living with Tanesha. That sounds like a wonderful arrangement for you. You could have her living with you while I'm at home, crying because you were not here. That's what will make you happy. You are just worried because you think that I may have found someone besides you. You don't even know if anything happened, but you are worried about it so you are going to do anything you can to put a stop to it. You were perfectly fine with all this before you heard that he was here visiting me. Why are you missing me now? You didn't even think about me before. You never even let me enter your mind when you were sleeping around or when you moved in with Tanesha. Also just for the record, he isn't scared of you anymore. You can threaten all you want but he isn't scared like he was in high school. He is a Navy man now, not a little scared kid facing a bully. Plus let's see how the judge likes it when you come to my house trying to fight my best friend. I'm sure that will look great in court. Please be my guest. That's what a real man does, right? He talks to a girl like she's not worthy of him. He mentally and verbally abuses her to where she starts to believe that she is nothing. He locks her in a room away from her children. He makes her believe that she is too fat to be with him. He makes her think that she's a horrible person. He even hits her when he gets mad enough. Your arrangement sounds like a swell plan. Seth, we are through. No thank you. I'm sorry that you miss me. I'm sorry that when you look at her it don't feel right because she is not me but Seth, you are the one that chose this. You made the decision to sleep with other women when you were married. You chose to throw away our marriage. There is nobody to blame but yourself. Thank yourself, not Trey."

"Why are you so angry? You are the one that just had sex with your best friend. You also threw away our marriage. We still had a chance until you allowed him to touch you and to do that with you. You threw us away. I always knew not to trust him. I hate him. I hate you also. You are both going to go to hell for breaking up a happy marriage. We could have worked this out, Hope. You are a slut."

"Seth, if it makes you feel better about what you did wrong by thinking that he and I slept together, go ahead. I don't care. I'm going to hell, huh? Well if having the best night of my life causes me to go to hell, at least I had one night in Heaven before I have to go there." With those last words, she hung the phone up on him. She was done and didn't have to justify herself with him anymore. She had not slept with Trey but she decided to let him wonder. It was not any of his business what they did anymore. It was not a lie. The night before had been the best night of her life. He heard the line go dead on the other end and slammed the headpiece on the receiver several times, cussing loudly as he did it. Truthfully he didn't want to get back with her but he wanted her to turn Trey away. He felt like she did not deserve to be happy. If he could not have her, he didn't want anyone to have her. Had they slept together? He wasn't sure why but it did make him mad that she may have moved on so quickly. He was her first everything and she was not supposed to move on. It was ok for him to move on, but she was supposed to wait on him and he didn't like it one bit that she may have already done something.

"What's wrong?" Tanesha asked.

"Nothing," he yelled angrily and stomped off.

Trey called her when he got to Houston and let her know that he made it safe. "I miss you already," he told her.

"I miss you too," she said. He could hear the smile in her voice and it made him very happy. Could this work? Was it possible for them to make it when they lived in different states? He figured that he would see how the weekend went and decide from there where to go with the relationship.

# Chapter 4

## Lonestar Concert

A couple days later, she got a letter on her email.

Dear Hope,

I have done some soul searching and I am happy with where we are now. I want things to stay like they are. This is what I want.

Trey

She smiled and was glad that he wanted what she wanted. Could this work when he lived thousands of miles away? Only time would tell. She was excited that he would be back that night though. They were going to the Lonestar concert. Lonestar was her favorite band so going to watch them with the person that she was crazy about was going to be amazing. He came back to town and got with her and her cousins as soon as he reached town. They had to drive all the way to BillyBobs in Fort Worth so they headed out early. On the way to the concert, she got to watching a train and almost ran into a Uhaul truck, scaring everyone in the car so they laughed about that the rest of the way there.

They got to the concert and he took her out on the dance floor before the band got there and they danced. Right before the band went on, she met a 7 year old girl named Dakota. "Hi, I like Lonestar. They sing I'm Already There and that song reminds me of my daddy because he is in the Navy. I sure miss when he is gone but that song makes me think of him and reminds me that he is with me even though he is off at sea."

Hearing that from this child tugged at Hope's heart. It reminded her that if she and Trey did make it somehow, that would be a big part of her life but she was willing to go through that to be with him. "This guy is in the Navy also and it also reminds me of him," Hope told her.

"Your daddy is a Navy man? Which guy is your dad? I want to meet him," Trey told her. Dakota pointed to her daddy and Trey introduced himself to him, where they got to talking about where they had been stationed and so forth. After they talked for a minute, the band came on and Trey asked Dakota's daddy for permission to dance with Dakota. Hope thought that was so sweet. Her dad said that would be ok and Trey asked Dakota for a dance.

"No, I want to stay here with my daddy. He hasn't been home long and I want to stay with him."

"I understand sweetheart," he told her. Then he looked at Hope and said, "I just got shot down by a 7 year old but I know a couple little girls at home that would probably dance with me if I asked them."

"I'm sure they would."

The song "Smile" came on and he pulled her out to the dance floor where he started to dance with her. He held her close to him and neither of them wanted to let each other go. That song ended and the song "Not a Day Goes By" started. Somehow as they were dancing to that song, she knew that as long as she lived, she would think of him every single day. He was someone that she would never be able to let go of no matter how many years went by. When the song "I'm Already There" came on, he sang it softly to her. He reminded her that no matter how many miles away he was, he would be with her in his heart. She leaned into his chest and felt a warm tear well up in her eyes and slowly slide down her face. She could not help it. She knew how hard it was going to be to give him up and unfortunately it was inevitable and they both knew it and hated it. When the song "Evertyhing's changed" came on, he sang that to her as well. He told her that song reminded him of her. "Through all these years, even though our hometown has changed, the way I felt about you never changed."

"I hope it has because we have kind of gone from friends to more than that."

"Yea but I always wanted that with you from day one so technically I have not changed the way I feel about you." After the words came out of his mouth, she felt herself start to blush.

"That's cool, sorry I didn't realize how I felt about your sooner."

"You are definitely worth the wait."

"Thank you."

The concert was so much better than she ever imagined the day that she had bought her ticket. She had bought her ticket thinking it would just be her and her cousins going but instead it was one of the greatest nights she would ever have. On their way home, Trey offered to get everyone a hotel to share but Della and Mark were ready to get home and truthfully so was Hope. She did not want to stop at a hotel. After dropping her cousins off, they drove to her house where they hugged each other for a little while in the living room. They were both tired so they decided to lay down together. That night, they did not stop at making out. They made love. The whole time, he never looked away from her but stared into her brown eyes and she stared into his green eyes. He pulled her so close to him and she felt the strength in his arms as they were wrapped around her. As many times as she had been with Seth, she had never felt anything like she felt that night. He kissed her the entire time and kept telling her how lucky he was to be with her. It was the most erotic moment of her life. After they climaxed together, he laid right there in her arms until the next morning.

The next morning, she got up and made pancakes. As she was cooking pancakes, he wrapped her in his arms and kissed her on the neck for a bit, causing her to burn the pancakes. She started laughing and snuggled up to him. Then there was a knock on the door.

"I'll get it," he told her.

It was Seth returning the girls. When he saw Trey, he balled his fist up and had a sour look on his face because it was very early in the morning so he knew that he had stayed the night.

Trey just flashed his biggest smile at Seth and then said, "Hey girls, we are so glad that you are home."

"Trey!" Desirae exclaimed and threw her arms around his neck. He picked up both girls and hugged them close. Hope had already told him about the conversation that she and Seth had about him but he didn't care. It was Seth's fault that his marriage had failed, not his. He wasn't complaining though.

"So Seth, how have you been? I've had a wonderful week. It is so good to be back home. I have missed everyone so bad," Trey said. He was halfway trying to make conversation but also trying in his own little way to rub it in.

"Freaking peachy. Glad your week was so freaking great," he said sarcastically. "Desirae, Kelsey, daddy loves you both. Remember, I'm your daddy, not him or anyone else."

Trey felt his lips turn upward just a little bit. He had not come to take the place of their father but he wanted to get to know them.

"Seth, I don't plan on trying to take your kids away from you. I would never do that."

"Well, aren't you a nice guy," he said sarcastically, pulling his kids to them and hugging them close. "I love you girls. I will see you both soon. Tell your mama that I will see her after Trey goes back out to sea. Tell her that when he walks out the door, I will still be around. He got what he wanted but I will still be here when he goes back across the country. She forgets that he is just going to be leaving her soon."

"Hey man, I want to get along. I don't want to fight with you Seth. Hope is a great lady and your girls are awesome. Thanks for allowing me the opportunity to spend time with them," Trey said, losing his attitude. "I'm sure that this isn't easy on you. If you ever want to talk or anything, I am here. I'd love to talk everything out if you are in to that."

"Save it Freshman. I will run into you when the girls are not around. I won't forget what you have done here. If I were you, I would be ashamed knowing I broke up a family." He cracked his knuckles then turned and left. Trey had truly tried to be nice and to lose his attitude but it was obvious that Seth didn't want to hear it. He was mad and was ready for a fight.

Oh well, he played with the girls for several hours, until it was time for him to leave to head out to Dallas to go back to the air port.

"I'm going to talk to your mama for a bit girls. You ladies want to watch tv?" Desirae handed her favorite movie to her mama who put it in the vcr and started it.

He and Hope went into the dining room and he pulled her close and hugged her close to him. "This sucks. I'm not ready to go."

"I know. I wish you didn't have to go."

"Just remember I'm already here just like the song says that we just danced to last night. I am the sunshine in your hair, I'm the shadow on the ground. I'm the whisper in the wind. I'm your imaginary friend and I know I'm in your prayers. I'm already there."

"That don't mean that I want to let you go."

He took her hands in his and pulled her to his chest. She laid her head on his chest as he held her close. She looked up into his eyes and saw tears in them. Wow. He was misty eyed. He took his hand and wiped his right eye. "I have to go. I am sorry. This is the hard part about my job. Right now, I wish that I had never enlisted in the Navy. It is taking me away from what I want more than anything in my life."

"You will be back and I will be here, waiting on you."

"I sure hope so," He took her face in his hands, leaned down, and gave her a light kiss. He hugged her close one last time, turned and walked into the living room where he hugged and kissed both of her daughters on the cheek. "I love you girls. Take care of your mama."

"Why are you crying?" Desirae asked.

"Sometimes when we truly care about someone, then our eyes begin to leak sweetie. I'm sad because I have to leave and won't be back for a long time. I am going to miss you all." Hope could not help it, the warm tears started to pour from her eyes.

"We will miss you too Trey and we love you," Desirae said. He kissed her cheek then put her back down on the floor.

He hugged Hope close one last time and then walked out the door. That was the hardest goodbye that either one of them would ever have to face. That next day, she got the phone call from him that he made it home safe and would be calling her. He gave her a phone number to Pearl Harbor, where he was stationed in case of an emergency and told her that she could call and leave messages for him. Then he told her that he had to go. This was so hard for them both. He would be leaving to go back out to sea for awhile the next day but neither of them knew that at the time. She did not hear from him for six weeks so she had written him a letter telling him that she would rather be friends than to lose him completely. She would have moved to Hawaii to be with him in a heartbeat if he had only asked but he never would ask her that.

In the letter that she had written to him to break it off, she had told him that she would never be able to leave Texas anyway because she was trying to make it easier on both of them to move on and stay friends. If she made it look like it was all her fault, maybe they would be able to salvage the friendship. That had torn his heart out but he would never tell her. There was no way they could be together with her in Texas and him in Hawaii. He would have asked her to come to Hawaii to see him soon but then he had gotten that letter. He was going to call her but he had been trying to figure out what he needed to say to her plus he had been at sea for the past 6 weeks.

He didn't understand why she had broken off the relationship. Everything was so perfect when he had gone to Texas and spent most of his leave with her. Where had they gone wrong? Everything was wonderful when they were there, so why did she break up with him? When he was at sea, he had decided that when he got home, he was going to buy her a ring and ask her to go to Hawaii and meet him there. He was going to propose to her and ask her and her kids to move there with him. He decided that he must have loved her more than she loved him. Well, it was better to have her as his friend than to lose her altogether. He needed that friendship as much as she did. Instead of talking about it, they both assumed that the other one wanted the breakup. The truth is that neither of them wanted the breakup but it happened anyway. They both just let it go because they thought that is what the other one wanted.

One day, she decided that she was going to save her money and go to Hawaii to see him. She was hoping that something would happen with the two of them when she went up there and that they could salvage the relationship. She saved $30.00 out of every paycheck and had about $650 saved up for a plane ticket and even told him that she was planning on coming to see him soon but then her friend came over to her house and told her that they were about to lose their electricity and she needed $450.00 or they would lose their electricity. Her friend had a little girl and it killed her knowing that she had enough money to help her pay her electricity and she felt guilty knowing that she had enough money to keep her friend from losing her electricity. She went home and got $450.00 from her Hawaii fund and gave it to her friend. Her friend promised her that she would pay her back and Hope told her ok that she could pay it out if she needed to because she knew that her friend was barely getting by.

What she did not know what that Trey had bought a ring and planned on proposing to her when she came down to see him. He wanted to spend the rest of his life with her. That day would never happen. Both she and Trey went months without finding someone else. His heart was broken that she was not going to come see him. He was the first one to find someone new. He gave up waiting on her. When that happened, she thought it was going to kill her.

Knowing that he was with another lady truly broke her heart but she was willing to go through it to keep him as her best friend. He was very open about his girlfriend with Hope.

His girlfriend's name was Julie. She was a very cute girl who had a daughter named Lindsey. He finally had gotten a cell phone and sent her some pictures of Lindsey and of Julie. She told him that she was very happy for him even though seeing the pictures of them together broke her heart. They had not been dating long when she got the call that she never thought she would get.

## Chapter 5

## A Happy Heartbreak

"Guess what. I am getting married and I want you to be at my wedding."

She almost dropped her cup of coffee. "What? You barely know her. Have you lost your mind?"

"I know that is what makes this so crazy. I am in love with her. She flew all the way to Hawaii to see me. I proposed to her on the beach. You should have seen her. She wants to be with me. She makes me happy. Can't you be happy for me please? She is an amazing mama. I get to be a step dad. I can't wait to meet Lindsey. I am going to be marrying her next month. I am going to fly to Texas and marry her. I get to meet Lindsey when I go down there. I can't wait."

"You are marrying her and have never even met her daughter? Trey, I am happy if you are happy but don't you think you are jumping in way too fast? Get to know her a little better before you marry her. Please. You jumped into it way too fast when you married your first wife so please do not make the same mistake."

"You don't understand. This is meant to be. I know that I will love her daughter because I love your daughters. Her daughter is a part of her so there is no way I could not love her. I need you right now. I need your support. Please tell me that you are behind me on this. I truly can't do this without you."

"Trey, if this makes you happy, I am happy for you. Congratulations. Wow." She meant what she said when she told him that she was happy for him but she was sad for herself. She felt a lump in her throat as she talked to him. She was going to have to give him up for good now. She would never hold him again. He could never be her boyfriend again. Could she let him go? "Let me know the date and the place and I swear I will be there no matter what or where it is." He was getting married in Texas so there was no way that she would miss it, even if she had to drive half a day to get there.

"I will be counting on it. I am going to come into town about a week prior to the wedding. Can I stay in your spare room when I come down? My dad really don't have a lot of room in his apartment and I feel really comfortable at your house."

"Yea, but there is something you should know. I have gone on a couple dates with a guy. His name is Kasey. He and I started seeing each other last week. He took me on a date and is pretty nice but it isn't serious yet. He has a really nice family and they are really nice to the girls. I don't know if I want to get serious with him. It is hard to get serious with him when I am still in love with someone else."

She noticed that he got really quiet. "Wow, congratulations. I'm glad he is nice. Lucky guy. You deserve it and so do the girls. If you are in love with someone else and he isn't in love with you, he does not deserve you. You deserve someone that is going to love you back," he said quietly, secretly wondering if she was talking about him or her ex husband. She could not help but think that him getting quiet was a sign that he still cared and if he still cared so much, why would he be marrying this girl? She also could not help but think about how she would give Kasey up in a heartbeat if she had half a chance of being with Trey. He perked up just a little and told her that he could not wait to meet Kasey. "I have to approve of him. I am the best friend and if I don't like him, he has to go." He could not help but wonder why all of a sudden he was sad and was overwhelmed by jealousy toward this guy. He was engaged to be married next month, but he was sad because she was moving on with her life without him. It did not make sense at all. She deserved to be happy. "I have to go. I'm gonna call and tell my dad about the news. Talk to you later. Love you Hope. Bye."

Then the line went dead. Had he just told her that he loved her? He could not believe that he had just told her that. He had to hang up right after the words came out because he was afraid of what she might say back. Who was she talking about still being in love with? She was his best friend and they told each other everything so surely she would tell him if she loved him, right? He had been in love with her since his leave and could not get her out of his head but this was the first time since the leave that he had told her because he was scared of getting hurt. She wondered what he meant by saying love you Hope. Was he talking about a best friend kind of love or was he in love with her? She was so confused. The phone rang and it was Kasey. She decided to talk to him for awhile and try to forget about Trey for now.

Forgetting him was harder than she thought because the next day her phone rang. It was Christmas Eve. She could hear crying on the other end of the line. "Hello," she said into the receiver.

"I want to be home. I want to be there with you and the girls. I am so sick of being here. I just wish I was with you. I miss you so much. This is my sixth year away from home."

Did he mean that he wanted to be with Julie? He didn't say that he wanted to be with her. He said that he wanted to be with Hope.

"You mean you want to be with Julie, right?"

"I want to spend the holiday with you, my best friend. I want to be back in Breckenridge. I want to spend the holiday with your daughters too. I just hate it here, Hope." She was so confused.

"If you want to be with that person, why are you marrying Julie?"

"I love her. I just want to be with you. It's just not the same. I can't explain it. It is different. One is crazy about me but the other is the one that I really want and need. Do you know what I mean?"

She had to be careful with what she said because Kasey was sitting right next to her on the couch. Even though she liked Kasey, she really truly wanted to be with Trey.

"Trey, what exactly are you saying? I am confused but truthfully in a way I understand because I feel that way too. I am the same way. Yes, Trey I understand. I want the same thing."

"Is that Trey? I want to talk to him and say hello," Kasey said.

"Oh, crap. Kasey is there?" Trey tried to clear his voice. "Go ahead and put him on the phone. I would like to talk to him." Why had he reached out to her? He had a fiancé and was getting married next week but would do anything to be with her even though he was getting married.

"Are you sure? You don't sound good. I'm worried."

"I'm fine, go ahead and put him on. I need him to know that he needs to make sure that he takes care of my best friend."

"Ok, here you go," she said handing the phone to Kasey. Kasey was not sure what to think about her being best friends with a guy but he wanted to talk to him to see what he thought about it. It was not such a bad thing if he was marrying some other girl. He could handle that because it didn't seem like Trey was a threat to him.

"Hey man, I'm Kasey. Are you excited about getting married? I have heard a lot about you lately."

"Yea, I'm excited. You have you a great girl there. She is the sweetest woman I know."

"Oh I know man. I'm wanting to get closer to her than we are. We have gone out a couple times but I kind of want to be her boyfriend. She's great."

"Yea, she is perfect. You will never find a better girl. If you ask her out, you need to make sure that you treat her right. If you don't you will regret it for the rest of your life." Trey said glumly.

"You are one lucky man. I could not imagine all the beautiful women in Hawaii. I would love to go and babe watch sometimes."

"Yea we have some gorgeous women here but my heart belongs to a woman in Texas so that is where I would rather be. Hawaii has taken the best part of my life away from me."

"Yea, man I hear you. My heart is sort of into a lady here in Breckenridge right next to me."

"I understand Kasey. It would be very hard not to fall in love with Hope." Trey said truthfully. Kasey looked over at Hope and smiled. He liked her but part of that was to let Trey know that he wanted a chance with her. He was truly cool with the fact that her best friend was a guy but he wanted to make sure that it was just friendship. "Well, man I will see you soon when you come to Breckenridge. I look forward to meeting you in person."

"Yea, likewise. Can I speak to Hope again please?"

He handed the phone to Hope.

"Are you ok? I am really worried about you? Are you sure this is what you want, Trey? Trey, if you are really wanting to be with someone else, you need to tell her. I am sure that she feels the same way about you as you do about her."

"I'm great. I've never been better. It is just really easy to get homesick. I will see you next week and a week after that, I will be a married man."

"Yea!" she said. She pretended to be happy for him. "You won't be homesick next week. See you then."

"Yea, see you." He hung up the phone and started to bawl. He cried for hours knowing that he would never hold her like he did when he went on leave. Sure, he was getting married to Julie but it was not the same. She was fun, beautiful, and was amazing, but she was not Hope. Even though she was sitting next to Kasey, she wanted to be with Trey. She wanted to throw her arms around him and hug him and tell him that everything was going to be ok. She wished that she had gone to Hawaii when she had the chance. She felt tears welling up in her eyes because the what might have been was killing her. She was glad that they were watching a movie in the dark so he could not see her tears in her eyes.

"He seems like a really nice guy."

"He is great. I really miss him. I couldn't ask for a better friend."

"So what do you think about being my girlfriend? I really would like that."

"Let's see what happens. I like you a lot." He leaned in and kissed her which was nice but it was not Trey's lips so it did not feel right. The next day she called Amelia.

"He's getting married. I am not sure I can handle this but I promised to go. Why would I promise to go? Why do I do this to myself?"

"Don't go. Don't put yourself through that. That is just going to be painful."

"I promised and being friends with him means more to me than the relationship did. I can't lose him."

"He will understand Hope."

"You don't understand. He gives me all the signals that he is still in love with me but he is marrying her. I don't get it. This is so confusing."

"What about Kasey?"

"Truthfully, if I had the chance to be with Trey, I would let Kasey go but I don't have that opportunity. Kasey is a nice guy so I might as well enjoy this."

"Why are you convinced that Trey is still in love with you? Are you sure that he ever loved you to begin with?" She told her what happened the previous night, how he was saying that he wanted to be there with her and her daughters. She told her how he was crying and reminded her that he cried when he had to leave her. "This is something that you can't fake. I don't know how to explain it but you can't fake this stuff. He still cares for me. I am not sure how I know but I know him so I just know."

"So, what are you going to do about it?"

"I'm going to enjoy seeing him next week. I am going to drive to the wedding, meet her, and I guess have to let him go. That unfortunately is my only option now. Best friends have to do that because they can't be a couple anymore once one of them gets married. This hurts. I hate this. I should be happy for him but I can't be because I am too sad for me."

"Don't go. Make up an excuse. Tell him your car broke down or that you don't have the money. It is going to be too hard on you to do that Hope. It isn't fair to you. It isn't fair to her either if he really loves you. How would you like it if you were marrying a guy and he secretly wanted to be with someone else who showed up at the wedding more than he wanted to be with you? It would hurt you very badly."

"If we are going to stay best friends, I will have to meet her. I might as well do it on the best day of his life."

"Ok, well, you know that I am here for you when you need me. Hope, you are going to fall on your butt. This is going to kill you and I can't stop you. Just know that when you do fall on your butt, I am here for you ok. I will always be here for you even if I don't agree with what you are doing in the first place."

"I know. It isn't like I killed someone. I just fell in love with my best friend Amelia."

"Do you need someone to go with you to be your moral support so that you have someone there with you?"

"No, like I said, I will have to get to know her and I want to be there for him. I will be ok. I'm tough."

"Sometimes you are too tough for your own good. Ok, I'm here if you need me."

"Well, I'm going to need you. I don't think that it has hit me completely yet."

"Yea, but when you see him and see her in the dress that you should be wearing and wearing the ring you should be wearing, it is going to hit you like a brick wall. My advice is don't go. You will regret it. Please don't do this." The thought of another woman wearing the ring that she should be wearing caused her to cry harder. "Yea but I will regret not being there for him more. He needs me. I gotta go."

They said goodbye and hung up the phone. She didn't know how she was going to handle losing him. This was going to be so hard. She already had to lose him once but this time it was for good. The week seemed to drag by as she waited for Friday to get there so she would be able to see him. They both were so very excited. As he was flying in, he had decided that if she showed any interest in being more than friends, he was going to stop the wedding. He could not help it. He loved her and wanted to be with her but could not wait on her forever. Hope had decided that if anything happened between them, she would do anything at all to be the one that walked the aisle with him but she could not do that at the cost of the friendship. She finally heard that knock on the door. She opened it and he leaned in and hugged him close to her.

Being in his embrace brought memories to both of them. It felt so good. He hugged her for about five minutes and she had to truly fight the tears back as he held her. "I have missed you so much," he told her.

"Me too. You are the best friend I ever had. I wish I had gone to Hawaii."

"Me too."

"So, tell me about her," she said pulling away. She had to pull away because it hurt being held and knowing that he wanted someone besides her.

"She is very sweet. She is funny. She loves her daughter so much and is a great mom and most of all, she loves me so much. I am glad that I found a woman that loves me like she does."

"She is a very lucky woman, Trey. I am happy you found the one that makes you happy. You deserve to be happy more than anyone I know."

"So do you. When I came on my leave, it was the best days of my life and I realized how much I needed our friendship and how much I cared about you," he said pulling her close again and hugging her again. "I'm sorry I just missed you so much."

"Your leave was the best days of my life too. I wish that we could relive those days everyday for the rest of our lives," she almost pulled him close to kiss him when the door opened and it was Kasey. What? He was not supposed to be here today. He was supposed to have to work late tonight.

"Hi guys. Hi Trey. I'm Kasey. Nice to meet you man."

"You too." Man this guy had horrible timing. Trey was about to kiss Hope when he showed up. Kasey went over and hugged Hope and kissed her in front of Trey and Trey decided then and there that he was going to get married. It was obvious who her choice was at this point. She wanted Kasey.

They all talked for hours. Her daughters were with their dad that weekend. Kacey decided at midnight that it was time for him to leave because he had to be up at 4AM for work.

"He is right. I need to get to bed also. Thank you for letting me stay in the spare bedroom." Kasey kissed her goodbye and told him good luck on his marriage.

"Thanks. It is coming really fast. You listen to me. You see this girl here? She is amazing. She is the sweetest, most loving, wonderful girl that you will ever have. Her babies are beautiful and awesome. You will never meet another girl as wonderful as her. You take care of her ok. If I find out that you hurt her or mistreat her, I will come back for you. I would take her in a heartbeat if I had the opportunity so you better take care of her."

"Ok, I understand. I don't plan on hurting her."

"Goodnight y'all. I am going to bed. I will see you in the morning."

He turned and went to the bedroom and the warm tears started to flow.

"Babe, um your friend is in love with you. Can you see that? I don't know why he is marrying that lady because he is in love with you."

"What makes you think that Kasey?"

"Can you not tell? He told me that he would take you in a heartbeat if he had the opportunity. He told me that there is nobody better than you. Sweetheart, your friend is in love with you, not his fiancé. You can see it when he looks at you."

"We are just friends. He and I are not anything more than that. He is marrying a different girl. Don't that let you know that he and I are just friends."

"The funny thing is this. I have a feeling that you care about him the same way but you are harder to read than he is so I will just believe that you are telling the truth. I am sorry baby but that guy is in love with you. I will see you soon ok. I trust you though to be in the house with him."

"Ok, goodnight. I think you are wrong but thanks for the observation. I look forward to going somewhere together tomorrow night after he leaves."

"Me too gorgeous." He kissed her and walked out the door. He was worried about leaving her there with her so called best friend because there was no doubt in his mind that this guy was crazy about her. He found it odd though that he was marrying someone else. She watched from the kitchen window as he drove away then went and knocked on the spare bedroom door.

"Come in."

"Hey, why don't you let me stay in this bed because it is not as comfortable as my bed and you can stay in my bed. I will give you my bed."

"How about this, why don't you and I sleep in your bed together and I will stay on my side and you on yours so we both get a good nights sleep."

"Sure, sounds good."

They both laid on her bed and faced each other and chatted for a long time. She did notice that he leaned in and hugged her tightly and they fell asleep that way. Going to sleep in his arms that night would just make it harder for her to say goodbye again that next week but it felt so good that she could not pull away. He never tried anything with her that night. They only slept.

The next morning, they both laid there awake, neither of them wanting to move to even go to the bathroom because they wanted to cherish that moment forever. He opened his eyes and just stared into hers.

"I am going to miss this," she finally said. "Your fiancé would be so upset if she knew how we slept last night."

"Truthfully right now I would not care. Last night was great and we didn't touch each other sexually so she should not get mad."

"Kasey would be angry too probably."

"He already thinks you have it bad for me. He was trying to convince me that you were crazy about me when he was here. You know how guys are when a girl has a guy best friend. He told me that he could tell that you were in love with me," she said smiling but also hoping that he would say something to her.

"Yea, I know how us men are when it comes to emotional stuff. Wonder why he would think that. Gosh, I hate to do this but I have to get up. I have to get on the road and get to her. You promise you are coming to the wedding? I could not do this without knowing that you are going to be by my side when I do it. I need you there."

"I wouldn't miss it Trey. That is your big day. I would not want to miss it."

"I'm kind of scared. What if this is a mistake, Hope? A part of me wants this worse than anything but a part of me is terrified that I am making a huge mistake. What if I am making a mistake? What if her daughter don't like me? What if I have the chance to have the love of my life for the rest of my life and I am blowing it?"

"I guess you need to ask yourself what you really want. Do you love her enough to spend the rest of your life with her? Get to know her daughter and see what happens. You have your entire life to get married. If you are not sure, tell her that you need a little more time. You are jumping in so fast. She would have to understand why you are scared."

"She has spent a fortune on this wedding. I already had her ring. I had actually bought it for someone else and never had the chance to give it to that girl. Is that a bad sign?"

"I just feel sorry for the girl that lost out on you," she said, choking back the tears. "That girl is the one that will regret it for the rest of her life Trey. She should have never let you go."

"Well, I kind of feel sorry for me for letting her go."

"You never told me that you almost got married to someone else. When did that happen?"

"It didn't. I never had the opportunity to propose to her."

"Oh, I am sorry but all I can say is everything happens for a reason. There is a reason that you never had the opportunity to propose to her and maybe Julie is that reason. Maybe she is your soul mate. You have to determine that. Did you ever tell the other girl that you almost proposed to her?"

"Not exactly. She knows that I almost proposed to someone else but I never told her that it was her."

"Trey, do I know this girl that you almost proposed to?"

"You know what, none of that makes a difference anymore. I am getting married in a week. I need you to be at the wedding for me. I can't wait for you to meet her. I need to get up and get on the road. I am so thankful for our friendship. We can't ever let that friendship die ok?"

"No way." She leaned over and kissed him on the forehead and got out of bed. She went into the kitchen and started to scramble eggs and cook bacon as he went to the restroom. After he ate, he hugged her tightly and walked out the door. He had almost told her but he was too scared to come out and say it. Well, he made up his mind for good. He was marrying Julie and would walk away from Hope and would never hold her like that again. He was determined that was the last time they would ever spend the night in each other's arms.

Right as he was leaving, he turned to look at her and began to sing Good Morning Beautiful. Then hugged her one last time and walked out. He could not help but notice the tears that ran down her cheeks. He understood completely because he felt like crying also.

That day Hope went to Amelia's house and told her everything that happened.

"You are right, he is in love with you. He was going to propose to you. You are the girl. He came out and told you that she knew. He just told you. Well, you have to make a choice. Either bite the bullet and tell him how you feel or let him go forever. It is your choice."

"Yea, tell him and lose his friendship forever or stay shut up and keep my best friend. I will just stay shut up. Man this really stinks."

"Have you ever came out and told him that you were in love with him?"

"Yes, not in so many words but I told him in a letter I wrote him when he went back to Hawaii."

"Ok, you can get on with your life then knowing that you told him and that you did everything you could do to be with him. You tried and it did not work out. You guys were meant to be. At least you tried.."

"Yea. At least I have a friend still."

That night she went out with Kasey and they had a good time.

"Did you tell your friend what I said?"

"About him being in love with me? No, I'm sorry but I don't want anything to be awkward between us. That would be too weird for us both. If he really is, then he would feel funny and so would I. I would rather keep it as just friends."

"I understand. That would be awkward. It is not worth you losing your best friend over. I don't mind that he is in love with you because I have you here with me. Did you guys ever have a romantic interest in each other? Did you ever date or sleep together?"

She did not think that it was important because that was so long ago and did not think it was any of his business because he was not around back then so she didn't think it was important to mention it now.

"He is my best friend. That's all we will ever be," she said, thinking that it was not exactly a lie.

"Well, that is a relief because that would be awkward for me. I will be honest, I had a hard time sleeping last night. I was scared that I was leaving you alone with him and something would happen."

"Nothing happened. We talked a little bit longer, went to sleep, and he left to be with her this morning."

"Did you want me to try to get off work to go with you to the wedding? You are going to have to drive about 6 hours one way to get there so if you want me to try to take off work, I will."

"Nah sweetie, you go ahead and work. I will follow his dad in my car up there so I won't get lost. It will be ok. Thank you for asking though."

"Ok. When do the girls get back? I want to hang out with them and play with them again."

"They are with their dad this weekend and he is going to keep them while I go to the wedding."

"Ok I understand. Maybe I can swing by sometimes during the week and play with them."

"Thank you for being good to my girls. You and your parents have kind of taken us in and been good to us this entire time. I appreciate it."

"Why wouldn't we be good to you and your girls? My mama is a sweetheart and she taught me to be nice too. I know that I am younger than you but I really like you and I like your daughters. Your daughters are precious."

"I know they are little bonuses. Trey always called the girls little bonuses."

"Sweetheart, are you sure that you are not into Trey? If you are, I guarantee that he would marry you in a heartbeat over his fiancé. It just seems like you two are meant to be to me. I don't want to lose you but it just seems like you really want to be with him to me. I just feel like your heart is with him."

"Kasey, Trey is a friend. He is my best friend so yes I want to be with him but we are not romantic. He is the reason that I was able to get through my divorce. He was the rock that kept me from drowning. He will be there for me through thick and thin but we are not lovers. Trust me." Technically she was not lying since they were no longer together.

"Ok sweetheart. I'm glad to hear that because it gives me a chance with you that I would not have if you were interested in him. I want you to get this wedding behind you then I would like to see us move forward with our relationship if you are willing. I want to be more than what we are now. I want you to be my girlfriend but not until after this wedding. I feel like you need to get that done before you will be able to move on and I know that he will need that because of how he feels about you."

"I'd like to see how this goes because I think a lot of you and I really like you and your family. You guys are the sweetest." He smiled at her.

"You are beautiful and I feel like a lucky man by getting the opportunity to spend time with you and your girls."

She smiled at him really big and thought that if she was not in love with Trey, he would be a great catch. It was just so hard to move on when her heart still was with Trey. Just a few more days and Trey's new chapter on life would begin and she would be forced to move on with hers because she would know for sure that chapter in her life would be over. She thought that in a way it would be a relief so she would be able to move on with her life but the night before the wedding would prove her wrong.

# Chapter 6

## Is This Really Happening?

The night before the wedding, Hope ended up going to Amelia's work and was a nervous wreck. Amelia was closing up and Hope was reaching out to her. "I don't understand. Why is he marrying her? He belongs with me. We had this great, amazing, wonderful weekend and it was the best days of both of our lives and he is marrying her. Why? I would move to Hawaii tonight if I had an opportunity to be with him. Why does she get him? I want him. I want to be with him. Amelia this hurts so bad. I am not going to the wedding. I can't possibly go and watch the man I am in love with marry someone else. I just can't do this. This just hurts way too much. I can't do this. I am not this strong."

"I don't blame you. I would not be able to do this either but you are the strongest person I know. I would just come out and tell him that you love him. Make sure that he knows that you are an option because I think that he will pick you if he knows that he has a choice."

"He would not pick me. He is marrying her. He is marrying her because he wants her, not me. Did he ever want me or was I just a notch in his belt that night? Does he even care about me?"

"Ok goofy, you are not just a notch in his belt. You are his best friend and truthfully I think he is feeling just like you are but he just don't know how to show it any better than you do so you need to just calm down."

"Calm down? How can I calm down? The guy that I have been in love with for years now is getting married tomorrow? I can't do this." She felt the tears start to come to her eyes right then.

"Hope, don't go. That would just be torturing yourself. Tell him anything to keep from going. You may have to lose him though. You may just be losing him forever this time. I know if he were my husband, I would not want him spending so much time with someone that he was in love with once. It is not fair to you, Trey, or his wife."

"He was my best friend before she even came into the picture so don't try to get me to feel sorry for her. I will think about it. I gotta get home. This is a public place and I don't want anyone to see me cry. I have to get out of here. Thanks for letting me break down."

"That's what friends are for. Please don't go."

"We will see. I can't promise you."

"I will call you after I get off work."

"No, I am going to be riding around, maybe go to the church to pray. I don't want to go home right now."

"Ok, I will be thinking of you. Are you sure that you don't want me to go because I know you are going. I know you too well to think for a second you will stay home. Do you need a friend?"

She smiled at Amelia because she was right. She knew she would be going before she ever said that she was not going to go. "I'm positive. I will put on my friend face just like I always do and be just fine in front of him. Thanks."

"And if you break down in front of him and an entire wedding party?"

"I am not going to let that happen. I am going to act happy by the time that I get there. I have made me a CD to listen to on the way there. It is all sad songs so I can get the crying out of my system. I even named it Depressing crap to get my point across. That way by the time that I get there, I will be able to act happy. I have 6 hours to get this out of my system and if it is too hard, I can walk out and drive off. I will be ok."

"Ok, you are much stronger than I am though. I could never do it."

"I have to accept his wife if I want to keep my best friend. I just hope that we can get along so that I can keep him in my life."

"I do too. If you two don't get along, I know you will lose him."

"She is going to love me. I will have to make her my friend too if I am going to keep him. I already know that." She drove around for hours, stopped by her church to pray and cried quiet a bit. This was going to be hard but she knew that she would be able to do it. When she got home at 11PM, there was six messages on her machine from him.

The last one said "Hope, I don't care how late it is, call me. This is important. I really need to talk to you."

She was going to call but wanted to get calmed down first. She had been crying too hard and was afraid that he would be able to hear it in her voice but then the phone rang. It was him. "Hello."

"Hope, what is wrong? You don't sound good at all. Have you been crying?"

She felt her voice breaking, "I'm ok Trey, what's up?"

"Did Kasey do something to you? Why are you upset? I'm your best friend. Talk to me. Please tell me what is wrong."

"I can't, what's up?"

"I wanted to tell you that Dad will be leaving at 7:30 in the morning if you want to follow him and my step-mom. They will meet you at their house and said if you wanted to ride with them, you are welcome to."

"I will meet them at their house. Thanks."

"Hope, what is wrong? You don't sound happy at all. What did Kasey do to you?"

"It isn't Kasey, Trey. I am just a little bit upset but I can't talk about it right now. I am ok, I will Call Amelia later and discuss it with her but I can't exactly talk to you about it. It is not fair to talk to you about it."

"Hope, why can't you talk to me about it? I don't understand. Did I do something wrong?"

"No, you have never done anything wrong. Look, I am sorry but tomorrow will be hard on me. I am happy for you but I am scared that she will not like me. If she does not like me, I lose you. Plus tomorrow is your big day and I don't want to talk to you about this because I feel like I am going to make your big day not as special. I am so happy for you but I also have to close a chapter in my life tomorrow. Please don't ask me anything else because I will end up crying even harder."

"Oh. Oh I understand. You are finally starting to feel what I have been feeling for months. I understand. Well, if you need me, you know that I am here for you. I always will be here for you. Oh, and she already loves you. I talk about you all the time."

"She does? She don't know about your leave a few years ago, does she?"

"Oh no and I want to keep it that way. That was the best weekend of both of our lives but if she ever knew that, she may not like you as much and it could be awkward for her. You didn't tell Kasey, did you?

"No, he is already convinced that you are in love with me so I could not really tell him that."

"All I can say is that he is a pretty observant man and he is pretty smart. Hey, I am getting married tomorrow. I can't wait to see you but I got to go to bed."

"Trey, wait."

"Yea? Amelia says that I need to just bite the bullet and tell you. Trey, I just want you to know that um well I love," she paused "our friendship and would do anything in the world for you."

"I feel the exact same way about you. Thank you for being you. See you in the morning Goober."

"Ok, I can't believe that our little Freshman is getting married."

"Goodnight." That next morning, she decided that there was no way that she could ride with his father. What if she lost it during the wedding? She would not have anywhere to run so she explained to him that she may leave earlier than he was leaving and that she needed to take her own car this time but thanked him for offering.

"If you want to know the truth, I always thought that I would be going to a wedding between you and Trey. My son was crazy about you and I can't believe that he isn't marrying you."

"I am in love with your son but he wants her so I'm happy that he is going to marry her."

"Well, honestly I wish that he was marrying you. I've always thought a lot of you and I know how he felt about you. Sometimes I wonder what he is thinking."

"Isn't it hard to go to a wedding when you are in love with the groom?" his step-mom asked.

"Yes, it is. That is why I am taking my own car. I might need to get out of there really fast and this way I have something to get out in quickly. This is just between us, right?"

"Of course sweetie," his step mom said. She understood. She could see it in Hope's face.

"I would never tell him especially since I was the one that brought it up," his dad told her then hugged her.

On the way, she bawled like a baby halfway up there. Once they arrived, she did pretty good. When she saw him, she felt happy. Seeing Julie made it a little easier because right away she liked her. Julie was funny, sweet, and a great person. She immediately thought pretty highly of Julie. Julie was very sweet to her and included her right from the start.

"I have heard so much about you. We are going to be just like sisters since you and Trey are so close. After she met Julie, she truly felt better about this. She decided in her mind that she could get on with her life that that she would be just fine. Yes, she would probably always love him but she would not have to lose that friendship because Julie was a great person and they became friends right from the start. She didn't have to lose a friend but actually gained a friend.

"I have heard about Kasey. Is it serious? I am going to throw the bouquet right at you. I'm hoping Trey and I get to fly to Breckenridge in a few months so that we can go to your wedding. We are leaving for Hawaii tomorrow because he has to get right back to work."

"It could be serious pretty quick but not yet. I haven't let it get serious yet. He is a sweetheart and he is good to my kids so I can't complain."

"Trey has been amazing with my daughter. He treats her like his own. He will be a wonderful step dad. I am so lucky."

"Yea, you are a very lucky lady. I adore him." That wave of jealousy was starting to come to her.

"He told me that you have been there for him through the roughest parts of his life and he has been there for you through your divorce."

"I would have never made it through my divorce without him. He had to almost carry me through it."

"That's awesome. He and I started off as friends also but it became more." They chatted for another 15 minutes then she had to get dressed for the wedding. She could not help but think that they may have been friends 10 minutes before he proposed to her because he had not known her for very long. She quickly waved that anger away from her mind.

Trey looked so good in his navy uniform in front of that church. He looked over at her and smiled that big grin that she had missed so much. She smiled back. Julie looked beautiful in her gown. Her daughter was adorable and they looked so good together and he looked so happy so she was able to leave there with a full heart. She didn't think that she would be able to walk out of there happy but she did. She did not catch the boquet that Julie had thrown her way though because she was not ready to marry anyone but Trey.

She drove home in silence until her cell phone started to ring. It was Amelia.

"How was the wedding? She explained to her that she was able to leave there with a full heart. I can't explain it. I know that I am in love with him, but seeing him happy made me happy. Even if it means that I can't be with him, knowing that he is happy makes me happy. I can't explain it but I'm ok. I feel like I will be able to move forth with my life now. I am going to tell Kasey that I will be his girlfriend and see where that goes. I think a part of me will always love Trey but I am happy that he is happy."

"I'm glad that you were able to get that closure. I guess you knew what you were talking about by insisting on going to the wedding. I thought it would mess you up but it sounds like it helped."

"Well if I hadn't liked her so much, it would have probably killed me but I like her and we are going to be friends so I think that everything is going to be ok. I am just glad that I don't have to lose him."

"Ok, I will talk to you later. Drive careful."

"Sure will and hey thank you for being here for me through all this mess."

"You are welcome. I know how much he means to you so being there for you through it was part of the job description of being a best friend."

# Chapter 7

## She Gained a Great Friend

From that day forward, every time that Trey called, she would talk to him and Julie. She heard an excitement and a passion in his voice that was not there before. Julie was a wonderful wife to him. One day, Julie called Hope.

"Hello."

"Did you know that my husband had been married before me?"

"Yea, why? They were not married very long and she cheated on him with his best friend when he was out to sea."

"I thought you were his best friend."

"I am but his best friend in the Navy. He came home from sea and caught them in bed together. It really tore him up. He didn't tell you?"

"No. He forgot to mention that. I don't understand why he would not have told me. Is there anything else that he forgot to tell me that you know of?"

"Nope, he has only been married one time other than you and she tore his heart out. She hurt him so bad and he probably just pushed it out of his head."

"Well, I don't get why his best friend would know and he didn't bother to tell his wife."

"Julie, he was not married to her long at all. He may have been married a couple months to her but that is all and in that short amount of time, he was out to sea for part of it so I can't tell you how much of a marriage they actually got to have. I knew about it because he brought her to Breckenridge once and I just happened to get to meet her. I bet he just forgot about it. That was a really hard time in his life."

"Well, my question is if he forgot to mention a wife in the past, what else did he forget to tell me about? How much do you know about his past? Like how many times has he been in love and all that?"

"Honestly, I don't know that much. A girl went to the prom with him when he was a junior just to get into the door then refused to dance with him all night. He and I were best friends starting when I was in the 8th grade and he in the 7th but when I turned 15, I got a boyfriend that was extremely jealous and I had to miss out on part of Trey's life. I put my foot down eventually and was allowed to be a part of his life again but I missed out on a lot because of my ex."

"Do you know of many girlfriends that he had in the past?"

"Not really. He is pretty private about a lot of that but I will tell you this. He loves you. He wants to be with you and he is happy with you. Anything from his past is just that, his past. It does not matter anymore. Nobody from before you mattered." Her words stung a little bit because she knew that she was included in that time frame and that since Julie had come into the picture, she did not matter anymore. That time would forever matter to her but not to him. She wondered if Julie knew about the relationship that they used to have but did not feel like it was her place to tell her and that could end up causing problems between them in the future or between her and Trey.

"Yea but it just really bothers me because he didn't tell me. I have told him everything. It kind of seems like he tells you more than he has told me."

"Like I told you, the only reason I knew about his ex is because he happened to come to town and introduced her to me. It did not last long at all."

"Ok. I am going to ask him about it later. I just don't understand how he could forget to mention her."

"I am sorry he never told you. I am not sure what to tell you but she hurt him very bad. He didn't love her anywhere as much as he loves you. I never knew him to love anyone as much as he loves you."

"Awe, thank you so much for that. I think that I needed to hear that right now. You are a very special girl Hope. I am glad that he has you as a best friend and I am glad that I inherited you. Are you still with your boyfriend?"

"No girl, we decided to just be friends. I am trying to go to school and work so having a boyfriend just takes too much time for me now. He was nice but the feelings just were not there, you know? Plus he cheated on me once and that is all it takes to quit trusting."

"Yea, I know. Are me and Trey going to be ok even though he didn't tell me that he was married before?"

"Look sweetie, I would probably be upset also that he didn't tell me but anything from his past don't matter anymore. I would not let it get me down. He loves you and you both very lucky to have each other so don't let the past come between you please."

"Ok I will do my best. Have a great day, love."

She hung up the phone and thought about that conversation. Why hadn't he told her about his first wife? Was she just fishing for information to find out if they had ever had a relationship? She would never open up and volunteer that information. She had really tried to like Kasey but could not make herself fall for him because of how she still felt about Trey. She truly wished that she could forget him and move on and find someone else but she could not help loving him. Kasey had been nice but after she found out that he cheated, she put a stop to it right away. She would always be his friend though. Kasey asked her after she broke up with him if Trey was the reason that she was breaking up with him. "Look, whatever I had with him in the past is gone. Don't worry about him anymore ok. The timing is really bad for me plus you cheated and I can't just get over that."

"I knew you had feelings for him. I kind of felt it that night. I understand. He is a good guy. I wish for your sake that he had not married that woman because you guys were meant to be together. I saw that the day I saw you guys together. I just felt it."

"I'm sorry Kasey. I was trying to overlook what I felt but you can't just let it go overnight."

"It's ok. I'm sorry I cheated on you. Hope if you are ever going to love again, you are going to have to get past this guy. It isn't fair to your boyfriend, you, Trey, or his wife."

"I know." He then kissed her on the forehead and they hugged bye.

The day after Julie had called her, Hope's phone rang, "Hey goober. I wanted to thank you for getting Julie to not be so upset with me yesterday. You kept her from divorcing me."

"No problem but why didn't you tell her?"

"I honestly don't know. I guess I didn't want her to know that I had a past. I can't explain it. Can I ask you a question. Does she know about what happened between you and me? You didn't tell her, did you?"

"No way. Let's keep it that way ok? Please. I don't ever want to lose you and if she finds out, she will be upset with me for doing that with you and I would have to lose my best friend."

"No I agree with you 100% that some things are better left unsaid between you and her but I do think you should have told her that you were once married because now she has that doubt in her head about you."

"I know but Hope if she ever found out about us, she would not allow us to talk. I can't handle that. You mean more to me than you will ever know."

"I know Trey because that is exactly how I feel about you. You are and have been my best friend for years so I think that our silence is the best thing that we could do."

"You know Hope, I still think about those nights all the time."

"You do?" She felt the lump come into her throat.

"Yes, I always have. Those days were very special to me and I will never forget them as long as I live. I'm sorry that I had to keep them just between us and not tell her but I will do anything to protect our friendship."

"They were very special to me also Trey. I can't ever explain to you how much they meant to me. It was harder than you will ever know to let them go."

He could not believe what he had just heard. Why had she broken up with him when those days were so special to her? He didn't understand. She also did not understand. "If they were so special to you, why did you break up with me?

"Trey, I had lost our friendship. You had not called me in six weeks and I thought that is what you wanted. I'm just glad that we got to keep being friends Trey."

"Hope, I did not call you because I had been out at sea for most of that time. I'm glad we got to stay friends too sweetie. You are the best friend that I ever had. Thank you for not telling Julie."

"What? You were off at sea? You did not want us to break up? You had called your dad. I thought I had lost you and our friendship. Those days happened before her and they are very special to me and you. If she found out about those days, it would not help your relationship so I don't see any reason to bring it up. It will be something between us for the rest of our lives. What she does not know in this instance will not hurt her. It is something that you and I can cherish and hold in our hearts. I will never forget what happened or regret it Trey. I will never tell my future husband either ok. Deal?"

"No I did not want to break up. I called dad and I tried calling you but never got through to you. I think maybe you were working or something. Hope, I wanted to be with you. I was planning on proposing to you when you came to Hawaii. I was in love with you and a part of me will always love you. It is too late now though. Sounds like a good plan on not telling them. It would not be fair to any of us. Hey I got to hop off here. I am about to hit the base. Talk to you later ok."

"Ok Trey. Bye." He had just lied to her. He was not on base. He felt that same familiar burning in the back of his throat that he felt every single time that he had to let her go again. He did not want her to hear that lump coming up. He loved his wife with everything but could not explain why he still was in love with Hope. Despite the fact that he had moved on and loved his wife, that leave was the greatest days of his life. He had just confirmed it. He was going to propose to her. As soon as they hung the phone up, they both broke down and wept hard. She was the one that he was going to propose to? The ring that Julie was wearing on her finger was supposed to be her ring. She cried for hours.

Months went by and Julie called her to let her know that they were expecting a baby. Hope was very excited about that. She was even more excited when Trey called her and asked her if she would be a God mommy to their baby. She could not wait to meet her little Godson and hold him in her arms.

When they made a trip to South Texas, she drove 6 hours to go see them and stayed in a hotel with her babies and a friend of hers named Dean Sellers while they were there. Dean and her had met when she and Seth were married and he was not busy that weekend so he had agreed to go with her in case of car trouble and to go along for the ride. She got the opportunity to meet Julie's family and get to know them when she was there. She adored them. They went to the park and let the kids play and she got to know his wife so much better. She knew for a fact that she would never do anything to hurt Julie or come between their marriage. She would never try to take him now. He was happy and that made her happy seeing him that way. She also adored Julie. She could not understand how she could still be in love with him and not show those feelings but he was worth it even though in the long run, it caused her all kinds of pain. At the park, Trey walked over to Dean who was pushing the kids on the swing and started to help him.

"Hey man, isn't Hope great?"

"Oh yea, I love her to pieces. My sister and her are really close. She was married to Seth and my sister is married to Troy. They kept her though when she and Seth got divorced."

"Oh wow, I have heard her mention you several times throughout the years but I never put two and two together. Don't you have a daughter that is the same age as her daughters?"

"Yes, her name is Ariel. She is beautiful."

"Awesome. So you are not interested in Hope at all? No romantic feelings?"

"You know what, Hope is a wonderful girl. I would date her in a heartbeat if she would give me the opportunity but there is someone from her past that she is still in love with so I don't have a chance with her. She is an amazing friend though. We have been through a lot together. I would do anything in the world for her and I know she would for me also."

"Who is she still in love with?"

"I really don't know man. Some guy that she was with right after she and Seth separated. He came to town and they had some special weekend together then he went back home and she has been crazy about him ever since. Lucky guy but pretty stupid if you ask me. She is a beautiful girl, a great mommy, and an amazing friend. I can't imagine anyone letting her go. If I had a shot with her, I would not let her go." Dean did not know that he was talking to the guy that had done it.

"Oh, I guess everyone makes their mistakes and maybe the idiot didn't realize how much she loved him until it was too late," Trey said. "Sometimes we close the eyes to our hearts when that is what we really should have been looking out of. I have known her for years and I guarantee you that the idiot kicks himself in the butt daily for letting her go. She is a great woman and she is beautiful."

"Yea, maybe so. Dummy probably don't even realize what he missed out on."

After they took the kids to play at the park, they all went out to eat then they went to her hotel room and played games together while the kids played with each other. Trey noticed that that twinge of jealousy came over him when he seen her with her friend. Her friend was a guy that she had known for years but had never had any kind of feelings for but he could not help but notice that he was jealous of him. Dean was able to make her laugh and she seemed happy around him. He really liked Dean and knew that there was nothing between him and Hope but it still bothered him some.

He had sort of taken his place as a best friend. Dean knew about her feelings that she had for Trey so he obviously knew more about how she thought and felt lately than he did. He caught a glimpse of her in the hotel room and it reminded him how beautiful she really was and how badly he truly missed her. He was going to make it a point to call her more often because he did miss her so much. Her smile was contagious as they were playing the game. She was laughing and having a great time. He could not understand how she could have fun and smile so much and not let on how she truly felt about him. If Dean had not told him, he would have never known that she felt that way at all. This game they were playing of trying not to show each other their true feelings was killing him. How could it not bother her at all? Maybe Dean just didn't know what he was talking about. He knew in his heart though that Dean knew.

That night as they were all sitting around playing the game, Dean realized for the first time in years that Trey was the one that she had fallen for. When she looked at Trey, Dean was able to recognize that look in her eye that she had the times when she had spoken about the guy she loved in the past. He felt like crap for mentioning it to him earlier but how was he supposed to know that he was the one? He decided to take it upon himself to make her laugh the rest of the night. He joked and made her laugh all throughout the night. Trey may have hurt her but he wanted to be the one to make her laugh and make her happy. He was all of a sudden jealous over Trey. Trey, Julie, and Lindsey left that night and went back to her parents home. Dean took a shower and she rubbed Desirae and Kelsey's back until they fell asleep. He came out of the shower and got on his bed since they were staying in a room with 2 double beds.

"Hope, are you ok? He is the one, isn't he?"

"Huh?"

"He's the reason that you won't open up and date anyone now isn't he? Is he the guy that you never stopped loving?"

"Why would you think that Dean?"

"I seen it in the way that you looked at him. That is what friends notice."

"Do you think that he seen it?"

"Truthfully Hope, he would be a fool not to see it. He loves you too, you know. I thought he was going to cry at the park earlier when we were talking about you. He made his bed and he has to lie in it. I think he is confused. He loves his wife very much and is a really good husband and father to her baby but he is torn because he still loves you also. He is a great guy. I really like him, Hope. I feel bad for you though. Sadly though I kind of feel bad for him too. He lost you."

She looked at him and he could see the tears welling up in her eyes. "I don't think I will ever move on because I will never quit loving him. It isn't fair. I should be her. I feel so horrible because I should not feel that way about him. He is married. I adore Julie. I love her to pieces and think of her as my friend but I will always love her husband. What kind of selfish, horrible person does that make me?

Sometimes I think it would be easier to just walk away from the friendship and lose him completely. I don't think it would hurt as bad as this does but I can't do it. I love him too much and he is my best friend. Dean, you said that he still loves me. How do you know? If he loved me, why didn't he try to stay with me? Why are we not together? I would have married him in a heartbeat." At that point, she started crying very hard. Dean got up and wrapped her up in his arms and held her as she cried over another man. He allowed her to just cry her eyes out on him. She was thankful to have his friendship. They had been through a lot together over the years. She had been there for him when he was trying to walk away from his drug use and thankfully he was able to walk away from it. He had been there for her when she let Seth go and now this. She would not want anyone else to be with her right at that moment as she cried on his chest. He could not help but think about how awesome it would be if he only had a chance to be with her.

"Hope, I know he loves you because he told me that he does. He told me that he kicks himself in the butt daily over letting you go. Hope, he did not realize how much you loved him until it was too late."

She laid on his shoulder, weeping until both of them fell asleep with her lying on his shoulder and his arm around her.

That night Trey kissed his wife and Lindsey goodnight and went straight to bed. He truly wished that Dean had not told him how she felt about him. Somehow it made it harder. Today was such a fun, amazing day and he was going to have to let her go again. Letting her go was always so hard. It always felt just like it had the day that he had to leave her after his leave. He could barely sleep at all that night, thinking of what he had learned. Had he made it where she would never be able to love again? That was not fair to her. She deserved to have happiness. Here Dean was a nice, funny, good looking guy and would love to have an opportunity to be with her but she could not do it because of her feelings for him.

He hoped that he had not messed it up for her for life because she deserved someone good, someone that would treat her the way that she deserved to be treated. If she found that person though, would she choose to stay friends with him or would she have to walk away? Would it be easier on both of them if they just walked away from the friendship? He could not bare the thought of losing her friendship though but thought maybe for her it would be best to let her go altogether so he would not keep her from the happiness that she deserved to have.

The next morning, Dean tried to talk her into not going to breakfast with Trey. "Hope, are you sure this is a good idea? You just spent most of the night crying over him and now you want to do it again? I don't understand. This hurts you so bad."

"Dean, it would hurt a lot worse if I have to lose my best friend so come on. Let's go eat breakfast with them so I can turn around and say goodbye again. I know you don't understand it. Neither does Amelia. I don't even understand it half the time but it is what I have to do. I would rather have him as a friend and be hurt by it than not to have him at all."

"Ok but Hope let me ask you a question. Do you think it is fair to his wife?"

"Well, as long as I do not act on my feelings and he does not act on his, I think it will be ok. If we acted on them, it would not be fair."

"I don't think it is fair to her at all. Her husband is a great man and loves her but he is also in love with his best friend and she has no clue. I am sure that he probably distances himself from her anytime that you come around. Think about it Hope. Ok well let's go eat then. I am starving."

"Me too and thank you for being here for me last night. I could have done it alone but it made it much easier having someone here for me so thank you. I will consider what you said."

"You are welcome sweetie. I will always be here for you, no matter what."

"And I will always be here for you too."

"I know that. That makes me a lucky guy to know that though," he told her and she smiled at him. He smiled back. Seeing her smile was so much nicer than watching her cry and not being able to take that pain away from her. They went to breakfast and ate then all went outside and said their goodbyes. She hugged Julie bye and kissed her hand then touched it to her belly to kiss the baby. She spoke to her baby bump then picked Lindsey up and loved on her. Trey hugged everyone and so did Julie then Trey grabbed her and hugged her as tightly as he could. He held her tightly and whispered in her ear that he wished that things could be different and that he hoped she could forgive him one day. She said huh and he just said "I'm sorry. Now leave it at that ok. Nobody needs to hear anything else." She hugged him back and loaded up her babies in the car and drove off. What did he mean by asking for her forgiveness? He honestly felt guilty about holding her back from loving someone again. That is why he was asking for forgiveness.

"You ok?"

"Yea, I'm going to be fine. Thanks again for coming with me Dean. He told me that he was sorry and hoped I could forgive him one day and asked me to leave it at that so nobody would hear."

"You are welcome. I am glad to have that opportunity to come spend the weekend with you. I am not sure why he would say that Hope. I think he said it because he loves you."

"I love you like a brother. Why would he say that he is sorry for falling in love with me?"

"Thanks I think. He loves you and can't do anything about it so he is sorry. That's my guess." He wanted more than a brotherly love from her but that would have to do for now. He started to laugh because no matter what, he truly cared about her and he would never turn his back on her.

"Hey, on the way home, let's stop by and go bowling or something Dean. My treat. Let's have some more fun before I take you home."

"Ok but we are going to listen to my metal on the way home and not your spoon slapping country. No, we can listen to your 80s rock cd."

"Fair enough." They played the 80s rock and stopped at a bowling alley on the way home.

"What's your favorite movie Hope?"

"I love Nicholas Sparks books and movies. The characters are so wonderful to their girlfriends or wives. That man understand the meaning of true love."

"Oh yea, I forgot you love chick flicks."

She would not know for months what happened in Trey's car that day when she left the restaurant.

## Chapter 8

## Brutal Honesty

A couple months later, she got the call that the baby was here. He was so cute and looked just like his dad. His name was Devon McDaniel. They sent several pictures to Hope and her daughters. The baby was so sweet. He was blond haired and had blue eyes. The baby won his heart over as soon as he saw him and helped to bring that relationship back with his wife that he had started to lose. When he seen her holding their baby boy, he fell deeper in love with her than he ever felt for anyone. It made things easier for him to talk to Hope because even though he would always love her, he was head over heels in love with Julie.

They decided to come to Texas to show off Devon to friends and family and they called and asked Hope if they could stay with her when they came. Julie told her that they would be glad to even sleep on the couch when they came.

"Nonsense. You guys can take my bedroom and I will sleep with the girls. They don't care. They like mommy sleeping with them anyway but I would love to have you guys stay with me." When they came down, they all gave hugs and she fell in love with her God baby. Devon had her wrapped around his tiny finger and the girls played and had a great time. She cooked for them and they all just enjoyed each others company. They stayed almost a week and just loved the entire time that they spent together. The day before they were supposed to leave though, Julie threw a wrench in the visit. He had gone out to visit some old friends that he went to school with and some teachers that he had growing up and Julie stayed with Hope when he was gone. As they were sitting there, Hope was playing with Devon and her daughters were at school. Lindsey was napping. "You and my husband must have a very close friendship."

"Yea, we have been best friends for many years now," she said.

"Yea, I know. You know the last time that we seen you, you were leaving the restaurant after breakfast and as you were pulling away, he put his head on the steering wheel and started to cry."

"Really? Like one tear?"

"No Hope, he bawled his eyes out."

"Did you ask him why?" Hope already knew the answer to that question but wondered what he happened to tell his wife that day.

"Yes and he just said that he was going to miss you. He said that was all that was wrong. Hope we stayed in that parking lot, waiting on him to stop crying for over an hour. I finally talked him into getting into the passenger seat and I drove home so he could finish crying. He cried for about an hour. He could not hold it in. It broke my heart because I have never seen him this sad over anything and those tears were real."

Julie was looking at her and she truly didn't know what to say. "I am sorry," was all that she could say. She was hoping that it did not show on her face what she was thinking. "I don't know why he cried over me like that. We are very close."

"Well, you are a sweet lady but I figured out why he cried like that. It was pretty awkward carrying his child and him feeling that way over another woman. I understand how he feels about you now. Luckily when little man got here, I think those feelings went away or were at least put on the back burner because our marriage got better after he came into the picture. He loves his baby boy so much. I can forgive him for having feelings for another woman, especially if it is you because you are an easy person to love. Look at me, I adore you but I want to let you know that neither of you better act on those feelings when I am in the picture. I trust you and I love you. I don't know what happened before I came into the picture and frankly, I don't want to know. That would kill me if you guys have a past and forgot to mention it so if you do, please don't tell me. I accept the fact that he loves you but as long as I am in the picture, you guys better not ever do anything. Are we cool still?"

"Thanks, I wouldn't do that to you. I am happy for him that he is happy and I would never hurt you or him like that. Thank you for not making him choose between you and me. I am not a home wrecker and would never take your husband or touch him when you are with him. Please know that. I am sorry about him crying," she said flatly. She felt so awkward and so bad. She kind of felt like a home wrecker even though she would never do anything with him now because of his wife. This was so hard because she loved Julie and adored her but she was in love with Trey and always would be. She excused herself and went to the kitchen to cook some food for everyone. That night, things were different. Just the fact that she knew that Julie knew killed her inside. Plus she could not get it out of her head. Why would he have cried like that over her? She didn't understand. She didn't think that he still loved her like that but obviously he did. If he loved her so much, why had they broken up? She went to bed really early that night to get away from everyone and told everyone that she had a headache. The next day, they all hugged each other bye. She turned around and went inside and bawled again praying that they did not come back. Why did Julie have to tell her about it and why was she nice about it? She felt like she deserved to be punished for her past with Trey. If Julie had hit her, she felt like she would have deserved it. She drove to Amelia's house and cried to her for over an hour.

"I just don't understand. Why did we break up if he still loved me and I still love him? Amelia, I don't get it. Why would he have cried like that if he wasn't in love with me? I told you that you can't fake those feelings. I just don't get it."

"Hope, why on earth do you do this to yourself? Every single time you and him are together, it kills you inside and you keep hanging out with him. I just don't understand."

"Amelia, it is better to have him as a friend than not to have him at all. I can't explain it but it is true. I love him too much to walk away."

"No offense but if I were Julie, I would make my husband quit talking to you. If I knew how much he loved you and he had been crying over you like that, I would have never came to see you. Even though he is not cheating, it is kind of like he is cheating. Even though you guys don't touch each other, you still are cheating in your hearts. If you or he cared about her at all, one of you would put a stop to it. It is not fair to her. How would you like it to be Julie in the relationship?"

"I can't Amelia. I am in too deep. Years of friendship is at stake."

"Ok Amelia but a marriage is also at stake. If he is in love with you the way that she is convinced that he is, you need to break the friendship off a little bit. It is not fair to her to have to compete with his best friend."

"Amelia, there is really no competition. He loves his wife. He is with her, not me. I am just the best friend. I will back off though. When one of them calls, I will answer and talk to them but I won't call anymore, ok. You are right, it is not fair to her. Gosh, why you do have to be so honest with me?"

"Cause that is what friends do, Hope. We don't hold anything back even if it means that we know that you could end up mad at us after we say what is on our minds. A true friend will tell you exactly how she feels. We are brutally honest even if it means that we may end up losing you because of the honesty. You need to be brutally honest with yourself about your feelings for Trey and for Julie's feelings."

"You could never lose me Amelia. That is just not possible."

"Good because I am just telling you how I would feel if it were my husband and you say that she is your friend so I am just telling the truth."

She went home after the conversation and was thinking about everything. Her daughters were off with Seth so she put a movie into the dvd player and sat down to watch it when she heard a knock on the door.

She answered it and it was Dean. "Hey, I came by to see how things went with Trey and Julie. I am kind of worried that I would find you crying again."

She told him about what happened and about what Amelia had said.

"Wow, that is hard. Well, how do you feel about that? I think that Amelia has some really good points there sweetie. I think that because I was the one to hold you until you got through it the last time and now she is the one that had to hold you through it this time. I can't help but feel sorry for Julie too. That would hurt and she is such a wonderful person."

"Yea, that is why I am going to back off. If they call, I will answer and talk but I am not going to make myself so available and I am not going to call him anymore. It is not fair to her or to any of us really. It is going to hurt though because I don't want to lose him. He is my best friend."

"Hope I know that I am not Trey but you always have me and you have Amelia. You know that we both love and adore you and will always be here."

"I know Dean but it is not the same. I love you and Amelia but I am not in love with y'all."

"I kind of wish you were," he muttered under his breath.

"Huh?"

"I didn't say anything. Hey, you want to go to Abilene tonight and have dinner and watch a movie or something? That would be fun and will get your mind off things."

"Sure, I would love to. That would be fun. Let me go put some warmer clothes on. I will be right back."

Dean got up and was looking at the pictures that she had scattered all over her living room. She had pictures of her babies and her friends, including himself and his sister. He did not understand why she could not move on and just forget about Trey. Sure he was an extremely nice guy and you can't force yourself not to love someone but seeing her hurt and cry killed him. She came out of her room and he looked at her and said "You look beautiful. You ready to put out tonight?" He teased her.

"Awe, thank you so much. That is very sweet of you but you need your eyes examined and of course not. That will never happen," she said grinning. He always teased her about sex.

"I wish that you could see yourself through my eyes. You would see what you are worth."

"Thank you so much. You are so sweet to me. It is great to have such a wonderful friend that is so nice and compliments you, especially when you are down. You are a self esteem booster to me," she said grinning.

"Yea, that's me," he said, somewhat sarcastically. He wished that he just had one chance to be with her. What would happen if he told her how he truly felt? He would just stay right where he was until she gave him some kind of a sign that he has a chance or one of them moved on. It was hard to want someone when they just wanted friendship and he was finally able to see what she felt for Trey. He was willing to sacrifice himself and his happiness to be with her when he wanted more and it finally made perfect sense why she felt like she needed to be with Trey. "You ready? I will let you pick out the movie."

"Yea, want me to drive or you?"

"I will drive. I want you to check out my new sound system in my car anyways."

"Oh no that means that I have to listen to your hard rock screaming music," she said and smiled at him.

"Tell you what, we will listen to my hard rock screaming stuff on the way to Abilene and your spoon slapping country music on the way back. Compromise, ok?"

"Sounds like a plan," she said smiling.

"You know that is the only thing that we do not see eye to eye on is our music. I like the amazing metal music where people are able to express themselves and their feelings and you like country, where everyone whines and makes you want to commit suicide. Those country singers are always either losing their wives, dogs, or their mom is in jail."

"Well at least you can understand that they lost their wives, dogs, and their mom is in the slammer. In your hard rock stuff, they just scream back and forth at each other. What on earth do you get out of that? Learning how to take your aggression and anger out by yelling? Yep, sounds like it is so much better than my country. I also enjoy Christian and pop rock. I love the 80s bands."

"Ok well I will also be honest, I love the older country such as Johnny Cash. I enjoy George Jones and people like that and I also love the 80s bands. They were awesome. Look, we just came to an agreement about music. I actually have some 80s and 90s music in my car. We can listen to that on the way to Abilene."

"Awesome. We did compromise on music. Nice. First time for everything. You like Johnny Cash and George Jones? So do I. You are looking more attractive everyday to me," she teased.

"There are a lot worse things that we can argue about than music so I think the music disagreement could be much worse. So if I look so attractive, you ready to go to bed now?" he teased her.

"Um not today. We have always gotten along really well except for our taste in music and how loud we listen to music and we are pretty good at compromising on that so we are cool. I am very lucky to have you as a friend even though you always try to take me to bed."

He opened her car door for her and she looked at him. "Since when have you been a gentleman?" she teasingly asked.

He grinned really big. "I've always been a gentleman but you never opened your eyes to see that because you are too busy worrying about Mr. Wonderful."

"Well I'm going to start seeing a lot more of your good side I guess because I am going to try to pull away from Mr. Wonderful a little bit. I don't want to come between a marriage. I also would never want her to think that I ever would. I am not like that. I never meant for her to even find out about our past. Is that bad?"

"I don't think it is bad. As for me, I don't care about the past. The past is the past and should not affect who you are with now. However I could see if he is still in love with you that it would be a big issue for his wife. I would have a problem if the woman I was with was still in love with her ex."

"Yea, I don't blame her. I am looking forward to this movie. Want to go eat something after we watch it?"

"Well of course. You already know where we are going to eat when we get there."

"Taco Bell," they both said in unison. They both started to giggle. They had been friends long enough to know what they both liked.

They talked the entire way to Abilene. They discussed their children, his sister, and each other. She asked him why he was not with anyone right now. "Well, I'm waiting on you to get over Mr. Wonderful so I can have a chance," he said, pretending to be playing but also wondering what she would say.

"You are so full of crap, Dean. You are probably just waiting around on one of my friends to come available again." In the past, he was known as a player and had spent a lot of time dating her friends."

He started smiling and assured her that he was a changed man and had no intention of dating anymore of her friends. "That's because I quit introducing them to you," she said teasing.

"Hey that isn't fair. I'm single and you don't want to introduce your friends to me? How am I gonna be able to find someone when you won't introduce your friends to me?"

"Go find your own friends Dean," She said smiling.

"That's not nice. I know that I was kind of bad in the past and that I used to have a lot of girlfriends but that is because I never found Miss Wonderful."

"Well, I hate to tell you this but she is married to Mr. Wonderful."

"Hey, I have never dated Miss Wonderful. You could hook me up with her and then you can have Mr. Wonderful. Sound like a good plan? She is a friend of yours and I would not want to ruin my reputation of dating all your friends."

She started to laugh. "You are crazy but hey you got me laughing." He was also laughing.

"It is good to see you laughing again Hope. You are so beautiful when you laugh. When you are crying, your face gets red, your eyes get puffy, and your mouth does this sad frown that looks like it is going to go all the way off your face. When you smile or laugh, it is contagious. You are beautiful either way though but I would rather see a laugh or smile any day."

"Well, I am glad that it was you that seen that scary looking cry face instead of Trey then. If it is as scary as you make it sound, he would probably never want to talk to me again ever and since you and I are just friends, it is ok for you to see the scary side of me."

"Hope, I'm not kidding here but have you ever thought of me as anything more than a friend? Seriously? I am a pretty good boyfriend when I am with someone. The one time that we kissed, I felt something, didn't you?"

"Huh? No. Dean, you won that kiss on a bet. I owed you that kiss because you won that bet but I didn't feel anything then. Did you? That kiss was not real Dean and that was years ago. You are like a brother if you think about it. Why? Have you ever thought of me that way? Besides I think we know each other way too well to ever date. I know about all your exs and you know about my feelings for Trey. I just don't think it would ever work out. Plus I would never want to lose the friendship we have or make it weird like it is with Trey."

"Yes, honestly I have thought about what it would be like to date you but I guess you think of me as a brother so I guess that would not work. Personally I think that knowing each other so well would make it better. I know that you can be friends with an ex because you are still friends with Mr. Wonderful and I still get along really well with a couple of my exes so I don't think that we would ever be weird if it did not work out. I don't want anything to be awkward though. I think that we are close enough in our friendship to never let anything come between us."

"Yea, but you have to remember you have dated most of my friends. That would make it really weird for us both and for my friends that have dated you."

"I don't think my past should really affect what you and I could have. I know that I have not been a saint in the past but when I really like a girl, I am faithful and I do whatever I can to make it work out. Besides if you ask your friends, none of them can say I was mean or a jerk. I just was never serious with any of them and they were not serious with me."

"Yea nobody ever said you were a jerk but that you were a player."

"I used to be but I am different now. I know that it would probably be weird though."

"Yea, it would. You are cute. I have always thought you were cute. You are hilarious and any girl would be lucky to have you. I know that you are going to make a girl very happy one day."

"You just really won't give it a second thought that you may be the girl though right?"

"I just think that we have way too many differences Dean. You like the hard rock, screaming stuff and I like country. You like loud music and I prefer my music soft. You smoke and I despise cigarettes and the smell nauseates me. I just think that we have way too many differences."

He was thinking that those things were all minor but did not want to argue with her about them. "Ok you are right. It would probably never work. Let's go see the movie ok."

They sat in silence watching the movie then they went to Taco Bell and he made her laugh the entire time that they were in there, just being himself. He was so funny. As she looked at him, she could not help but think about how cute he really was but she just didn't see him as more than a friend. They talked the entire way home. When he got her to her house, he walked her to the door and teased her about a goodnight kiss. She grinned really big and leaned over and kissed him on the cheek and gave him a big hug. "Goodnight Dean. I had a great time."

"Awe, I'm never washing this cheek again. Me too Hope." He went back to his car and decided that he wanted to stay friends but that he needed to move on with his life. He really liked her but he truly wanted to have a girl that he could get serious with and he knew that would never happen with Hope. He had gotten those feelings for Hope when he had won the bet and gotten the opportunity to kiss her. Those feelings had never gone away but even though he looked at that kiss as something real, she only seen it as the stakes of him winning the bet. He had bet her that she and Kasey would not work out and she thought that they would. He had told her that Kasey was too young and it would never work but she thought that it would so he had bet her a kiss if he won and he would buy her a steak dinner if it worked out. When it did not work out, he had gotten the kiss he had wanted for a long time. Now he could not help but think that if he had never kissed her, he would have never started to have feelings for her. He didn't regret the kiss though because he really had wanted to kiss her for a long time.

# Chapter 9

## Her Own Worst Enemy

Hope soon met a man named Tim Sealey. He seemed like a really nice guy and was great to her daughters. She was working at the local prison as a nurse and he was a correctional officer there. A mutual friend had introduced them and she agreed to go out on a date with him. She fell for him really fast because he was so good to her daughters and that meant so much to her. They dated just over a year when he proposed to her and she said yes. Right after she said yes, a nurse that she worked with told her that she did not see them working out.

"Can I be honest with you Hope? I don't see you with Sealey at all. You guys barely speak up here, you don't laugh, he is all professional, and I just don't think that he is meant for you. There is another guy that is working here that I think would be perfect for you."

"Who are you talking about Mrs. Watson? Who on earth do you think I should be with?"

"Mr. Sellers. You guys laugh, you play, you get along great, and he really seems to like you. He is really nice."

"No offense Mrs. Watson but that will never happen. He is my best friend. He is like a brother to me and you must be smoking crack to think that we are meant to be," she said laughing. Mrs. Watson died laughing.

"I'm not smoking crack but it don't take a rocket scientist to see that you guys really like each other. He makes you laugh all the time and you both are always happy around each other. I think that one day he will quit being a brother type guy and become the guy for you."

"No way. I know him too well. Plus he has dated all my friends and that would be weird."

"Well knowing someone that well and being best friend with them makes the best relationships. One day you will laugh with him about the fact that he dated all your friends. One day all that won't matter anymore."

"I know I have had that in the past and you can end up losing the friend eventually. It makes it awkward when you are around each other after you have a past."

"Yea but every relationship is different. If it did not work out with Sellers, I think that you guys would still be friends. You are too close to not be friends."

"Well Mrs. Watson, there is a huge problem with your theory. Sellers has a girlfriend now. Don't think that will ever happen even if we wanted it to."

"Oh rats, I did not know that."

"Yep he is with someone now."

"Ok I guess I was wrong about him being the one for you then. I'm sorry."

"It's ok. No skin off my back. He is a great guy and he has been my best guy friend for years. I think that is the attraction that you see. Years of knowing each other and a really great friendship but that is all."

"Maybe so but I swear I see it every time that you two are together. If he has a girlfriend though then I guess I was wrong. It has been known to happen from time to time." They both laughed.

One day Hope got a call from Trey after about a year of not hearing from him. He did not seem like himself. She and Tim were already having marital problems after a few months of being married. Trey had known about Tim because she had emailed him and Julie letting them know what was going on but they had not spoken about it. "What is wrong Trey?"

"She left me. I feel like my entire world has caved in. I think she is messing around with another guy. I was off at sea again and there were several posts between her and another guy on Facebook. I don't care anymore. I love her and always will but I just don't care anymore. I miss you. Why haven't you called lately?"

"You have not called either. I was trying to give you and your wife some space and time away. I also was trying to be a good wife to Tim but I don't think that is going to work either. I don't understand what happened? Julie loves you so much. What happened?"

"I came home from being out to sea and she was different. She seemed like she just did not care about me anymore then I started seeing these posts on her face book from another guy. So I started to look at his face book and she was posting on his wall too. When I was gone, it seemed like they spent a lot of time together so I asked her about it and she got mad and deleted me from her Facebook and blocked me. He blocked me too but I think that they were messing around. Just the posts they left made me think that they were messing around. What is the deal with you and Tim?"

"We just have our differences. We argue a lot and I don't think it will work out. We were married a couple months and then he just quit talking to me and watches porn all the time. Things are just different. We live in the same house but when I try to talk to him, he don't say anything. He just looks at me. I don't know, it is weird. Honestly it feels like I live with a stranger."

"She is moving out next week. We just are not working out. I really need my best friend as soon as possible. I miss you."

"I miss you too. Tim is still here but I don't see us working out either. Can you take a leave?"

"No I'm stuck here. Hope, try to talk to Tim. Try to get him to talk and open up. I don't want to see you hurt again."

"I'm sorry. I'm here for you and always a phone call away. Wish I could be there for you but you are so far away from Texas."

"Yea I know. Hey I will talk to you soon. I have to go. You have my number. Call me."

"Ok you too. Talk to you soon."

A couple days later, Tim came home and told her that he did not want to be with her anymore and that he was not happy and wanted to leave. He left that night. A week later, Julie moved out of Trey's house and went back to her mom's house in Texas.

Hope wanted to be there for him the way that he had been there for her when she was facing her divorce. She had a little bit of money put back and went online and priced a plane ticket. She could pull it off so she called him and asked him if he could pick her up from the airport in a few days and he said yes he could. She bought the ticket and booked her a room at a Motel Six in Charleston, South Carolina. She wanted to be a good best friend for him and he needed that in his life.

The next day she went to work and told Dean what she was going to do. "Don't tell Tim. He will be furious. He thinks that I am just going to the coast with my family. I really am going to the coast but first I'm flying up to see Trey."

"Have you lost your mind? Sweetie, don't you realize that he is single now? He is going to get you up there and take advantage of you and your heart. He knows that you are in love with him and he is going to get what he can out of you. He is going to hurt you again. Please don't go. Hope, I have never asked you to do anything but I am asking you not to go."

"No I'm going up there as his friend. That is all. Now if he wants to be with me, I will be with him in a heartbeat. He is single and I am single. It happened at the same time. Don't you see that as a sign? Stuff like that don't just happen by chance. He has been in love with me for years and I have a chance with him again. I promised Julie that I would not touch him while she was in the picture and she is not in the picture anymore. She left. She has another man. She left him. Tim left me. This happened days apart. I think that this is a sign."

"Hope, it is a sign alright. It is a sign of trouble. He is going to break your heart and I won't be there to pick you up this time."

"He won't break my heart this time Dean. We are going to be there for each other and help each other through a hard time. That is all. I am not going to sleep with him again unless he is into something more. I am not going to be a friend with benefits and he would never use me for that. If he wants to be with me though, I am not going to let the opportunity pass by this time. I know in my heart that it is going to work out this time. Dean if I had gone to Hawaii, I would have been the one that he married but I didn't go."

"Yea and you would now be facing your third divorce instead of your second Hope. Please don't be stupid. You and I both know good and well that if he wants to sleep with you, you won't be able to say no."

"Dean, that hurts and you don't know that."

"Ok, I will shut up. Have fun but please don't let him hurt you again. You don't deserve that crap."

"I am so glad to have you as my friend," she said walking around the counter and giving him a big hug. "Promise me that you will always be here for me."

"I just don't want to see you get hurt again and I have a feeling that it is coming. Hope, I will always be your best friend. You are too good a friend to let you go. I'm sorry I spoke my mind."

"No, this is going to be fun. I am going to love this. I give you my word. He won't hurt me again. I am going up there as his friend only but if something happens and he wants more, I'm not going to fight it but if it does, this time it will be for real. It has to be."

He just shook his head.

"How's your baby?"

"She is growing. My girlfriend is doing great. I think that I am going to ask her to marry me. I think that it is time to settle down for a change. She is a good girl and she loves me very much."

"I never thought I would see the day that you got married but congratulations. That is awesome. She is a lucky lady."

"Yea that makes two of us. Thanks. I'm going to go into this marriage 100 percent. I want this to work. I don't want to get divorced. I want it to work out, Hope. I don't want to be a statistic. I am going to treat her like a princess. I want her to be happy the rest of her life. She is carrying my child. I owe that to her."

"Wow. I have never seen this side of you. I have never seen you commit to someone. That is awesome Dean." For a second, she felt a small twinge of jealousy. Here was a guy that she could have been with that was determined to treat his wife like a princess. That was how she always wanted to be treated. Where did that jealousy come from? She felt like she had lost her mind. She could not remember a single time that she had been attracted to him so why would she be jealous of his fiancé? That just did not make sense.

"Hey, what happened between you and Sealey? I thought you guys were happy. I've always liked Sealey. He is a good officer and seems like a good man. You had seemed happy together the last time that we all hung out Hope."

"We were happy at first. I don't know. He started watching porn all the time and never wanted to touch me and got where he would not even speak to me. Things have been hard at home. I have a teenager now and they are difficult but I never thought that he would be that way. If I spoke to him, he would just look at me. It is kind of like we were strangers living under the same roof. He came home one night and said that he had made a mistake and wanted to leave. So I told him that I think we needed to get a divorce. He came back one night and told me that he still loved me and we made love and then he left and went back to his house. He made it seem like he wanted to work things out that night but when I called him the next day he told me that he just wanted sex and did not want to work things out. I will always care for him but after that night, I'm done. That hurt really bad. He is a good guy but just not the guy for me."

"Can I be brutally honest with you as a friend? I am scared for you that if you fly to South Carolina this guy is going to do the same thing. He will use you for sex then you will be in the same stinking boat you are in now. I understand if you get mad at me but I am saying this as a friend and I am trying to keep you from hurting yourself. You are your own worst enemy Hope. You always have been."

"I don't plan on sleeping with him again, Dean. I am just going there to be his friend. If something happens as far as a relationship is concerned, then that will make the trip sweeter but I am only going as a friend."

"What will happen if you do sleep with him and then you have to lose him again Hope? Do you really want to go through that torment again? Do you really want to stay awake at night crying all night over a guy. You had more passion for this guy that you ever gave to Sealey. That may have been part of why you and Sealey did not work out. You were never able to give 100 percent of yourself to him because you are still in love with your ex." She could not help but remember that Kasey had told her the same thing when they broke up.

"Well, I guess I will cross that bridge when I get there. Plus I have you and Amelia to fall back on and to cry to if that happens right?"

"You always have me and I know Amelia will always be there for you as well. We just don't want to see you get hurt again."

Just then an offender walked in and they had to quit talking. She was busy with offenders the rest of the afternoon but Mrs. Watson did notice that Dean had a sad look on his face. "Are you ok Mr. Sellers? You look like someone just shot your best dog."

"Oh yea I'm fine Mrs. Watson. I just adore Hope and I don't want to see her get hurt again. She has been hurt enough over the years but she just won't listen to anything that I have to say. She has been hurt way too many times and she is her own worst enemy. I would do anything in the world for her, but that drives me crazy about her. You know what I mean?"

"Oh I know. I tried talking to her before she married Mr. Sealey and told her that he was completely wrong for her and that I thought that she would be better off with you but she didn't listen to me then."

He kind of chuckled. "You know, I always liked you Mrs. Watson. Yea, I always thought that we would be great together but she always looked at me like a brother instead of a boyfriend. She always said that our taste in music is too different for us to be together. Plus she says that she knows me too well to be with me as a girlfriend. I can kind of understand that part. I used to be a player and I have dated all her friends so I can see her being worried about my past. Plus now I am happy. I am going to propose to my girlfriend. I am going to be a father soon in a couple months. I am going to go into this marriage 100 percent. I don't want to mess this up. I want this to work. I will always be there for Hope though."

"Good for you. I hope it works out for you and that you guys last forever. You are a nice guy and deserve it. I'm not sure what we are going to do with our girl in there because I don't want to see her get hurt again either but I am worried that it is coming."

"She is definitely her own worst enemy. She always has been."

"I guess we all have to fall flat on our face a few times before we can pick ourselves up and walk."

"Yep. You know she is a good girl. She is a real sweetheart and she loves with everything inside her heart. She is not an easy girl or anything like that. She has just made mistakes with choosing the wrong men. Her first husband was very mentally and verbally abusive. I know him and he was mean to her. Then she has been in love with this guy that she is flying to go see for years. Man I see why she fell in love with him and I see how he has messed with her heart over the years. He did not do it to be mean though. He truly loves her too but he got married and he was trying to do the right thing this whole time. I think that he was confused and did not know what he wanted. That just confused her so much more. She did everything she could to remain friends with him and was even friends with his wife also. This could be wonderful for her because he does love her. I seen it when I rode with her to South Texas to see them with her. He was crazy about her but he could not have her anymore than she could have him. I just feel in my heart like this is going to be a huge mistake and this is going to be a big speed bump that she is going to have to cross again."

"Mrs. Watson, please whatever we talk about stays between us ok? I don't want Mr. Sealey to find out that she is flying off to see another man when their divorce is not final yet."

"Sellers, I don't even like Sealey," she said with a big grin across her face. "I have seen the way that he ignores her and pretends that she is not even there."

"Well I like the guy but I got mad at him after he slept and made her believe that he wanted her back, he don't deserve her."

"Me too Sellers. At times like this, we just need to pray for her and turn her over to God because there is nothing we can do."

"I guess so." he said.

# Chapter 10

## The Weekend

She had butterflies in her stomach as she boarded the plane that would take her to Trey. He was going to meet her at the airport when her plane landed and pick her up. She was full of emotions. The butterflies danced in her stomach from excitement. She was worried, wondering what was going to happen, concerned about him and how he was doing since his wife left, but mostly fear of the unknown. She could not imagine the agony of losing him again. Would that happen? Was she truly setting herself up for failure like Dean predicted? He was right about one thing, she was truly her own worst enemy. Was she a horrible person for going to see a man that was still married even though it was over and his wife had moved on and was seeing another man already? She was also still married but it was over. Tim had already started dating a counselor at work so it was done. She sat in her seat and watched out the window as the plane took her to the unknown, to the comfort of her best friends arms, and to the possible destruction of herself. Halfway through the flight, she wished that she could turn around and go home but it was too late to turn back now. Trey would be meeting her in approximately one hour.

When she arrived, she grabbed her bags and walked to the restroom to check her looks. She applied some fresh powder to her face and then said a silent prayer. She was terrified that he would want her like he did before. She was more terrified that after everything that they went through that he would not want her. As she was pondering these thoughts, her cell phone rang.

"Where are you goober? I'm waiting outside the gate for you and I see that your plane landed."

"I will be right there."

He told her what gate to go to and she found it then walked out of it. He immediately scooped her up in his arms and gave her one of his big gorilla hugs that she loved so much. "Come on. Let's go. What hotel are you staying at?" He was wearing his Navy uniform and he looked so good in it.

She told him the name and location of her hotel and he jumped in the car and headed that direction.

"Thank you for picking me up. I'm so glad that I am here and get to see you."

"Oh you are welcome. Thanks for coming out to be my rock for a change. I need my best friend through this. I am so glad you came."

"How are the babies?"

"They are great. How are the teenagers?"

"They are a handful but I love them," she said grinning.

"Yep, they are supposed to be. You having teenagers makes me feel old. I played with them when they were just babies. They always have been little bonuses to an already great package," he said smiling.

"I'm so glad that I am here. We are going to have a great time."

"Yea, I can't wait to show you around. Charleston has a lot of history and is an amazing city. So, how is everyone in the big town of Breckenridge?"

"It's Breckenridge, nothing really ever changes."

"That is what I like and miss about it. I would love to go back home. How is everyone?"

She started telling him about how all their friends were doing and about who had passed away since they had last spoken. She told him that she had seen his dad at the store the week before and that he was doing well. She also updated him on who had gone to jail or prison from their hometown.

"Wow, I thought you said that Breckenridge never changes."

"Breckenridge does not change but the people there have a tendency to change from time to time."

He snickered a little bit. "Now I do have to work some when you are here but I will be around quite a bit. I took off as much as I could but I do have to work some. Also I am on call so it is a possibility that I may get called out even though I am off a couple days."

"I understand. Work is important."

"Yea sometimes I hate it though."

"Me too. I love my job for the most part but it gets old from time to time."

"So are you and Tim over for good or are you guys just taking a break?"

"It is over. He has already filed for divorce. He is seeing another woman already. What about you and Julie?"

"It's over. We have not filed for divorce yet but she already has another boyfriend and she has moved back to Texas to live with her mom. I hate it for the kids but you are lucky. You and Tim did not have any babies together so you are able to just walk away."

"Yea but the hard part is that the girls loved Tim so they are having to go through a divorce. I would rather it happen now though than later because I don't want them to go through years of him being like a dad to them then leaving."

"Yea that has to be hard for them. I am glad that he was good to them Hope. They needed that. Lindsey looked up to me as her dad. She knows her real dad but he barely ever saw her. One day Julie took her to see him and she was excited that she was going to get to see Daddy because I was out to sea and when she saw her biological father, she told her mama that is not the daddy she wanted. When Julie told me, it broke my heart for her. This divorce stuff sucks. I hate it. I truly wanted this marriage to work out. I don't understand why I always fail at this."

"I know. I feel the same way. I think that neither of us have been with the right person yet and that is why it never worked."

He looked at her, grinned from ear to ear, took her hand in his, and kissed it. "I know that you are right about that. I'm so glad that you have been in my life all these years. No matter what, you have always been here for me. Thank you for that."

"I wouldn't have it any other way, Trey. You were my rock that kept me from drowning when I divorced Seth and now it is my turn to hold you up."

"The truth is that right this second, I'm doing great. Here I am with my best friend in the world who happens to be a beautiful lady in a beautiful city. We are going to have a blast while you are here."

"Thank you for the compliment. You have always been super sweet."

"Just speaking the truth," he said, pulling into her hotel. He helped her unload her bags.

"Hey, I'm going to have to go to Wal-Mart and get some shampoo and stuff. They don't really like you bringing stuff like that on the plane. That can slow you down when you are trying to get through."

"Sure no problem. There is a Wal-Mart about a block away. The beach is about a mile down the street, and I have several places to show you. If I happen to be working, they have cabs all over the place that will be glad to take you wherever you want to go."

"Awesome, Let's go have some fun then. Are we going to the beach today? Do I need to put on my swimsuit?"

"We will probably go there tomorrow. I have other plans for today so don't worry about your suit. Plus I have to go to the base and get my suit. I will go grab my suit when I take you to Wal-Mart so we can take care of two things at once."

"Awesome. How far is your base?"

"About five miles from here. Come on, let's go see some sights."

He took her to the huge, beautiful suspension bridge. It was breathtaking. A stranger took a picture of the two of them in front of the bridge. He took her to the mart where the slaves used to be brought in by boat and explained to her that Charleston had a history for being a slave trade town. That made her sad to think about all the people that had been forced to leave their homes, families, and be forced to work or beaten. "That's sad," she said. He shook his head in agreement. He took her down a street that he referred to as Painted Row and explained that the owners of the homes painted the houses different colors so that the slaves would know which one they worked at. That was pretty neat to her and the house were really cool how they went from one color to the next all the way down the street. The houses were huge and beautiful.

He took her to the Fort Sumter National Monument and explained to her that the first shots of the civil war was fired there. They went to the museum and learned more of the history. It was crazy that such a beautiful place could have such a horrible history. There was so much to do here. She was truly going to enjoy herself while they were here. There were tons of restaurants and attractions, a horse and carriage ride to explain more of Charleston's history, and so much more to do. They walked out and overlooked the water. "It is so beautiful," she said. "I love the ocean so much. I wish I lived closer to it."

He grinned and kind of chuckled. "It is the ocean. I love it but I get to see it daily, remember? Sometimes I am actually under it."

She smiled. "I forget about that. I stand in awe when I look out there and no matter how far I look, I don't see land. I still feel amazed, knowing about the life under that water. I still feel like a little kid looking out at it. It is so beautiful and amazing."

"When I first joined the Navy, I felt the same way but try going out there and being under it for months at a time with nowhere to go but around the submarine that you are stuck on. It tends to make you look at it differently. There were times when we would come up to the top and they would let us jump into the water and swim but not very often. I used to look at the ocean in wonder but honestly I don't like it as much as I used to. I still love it but it is different to me now."

""I'm sure you do. I would probably hate it if I had to be stuck in it for months at a time! Well, you are still going to take me to swim in it when I am here, right?"

"Of course, I would not dare cheat you of part of your Charleston experience." He grinned at her. "Hope, this is your time and we will do anything you want to do as long as I am not at work."

"Sounds great."

"I love the Navy Hope. It has been a great job but it gets so old. Especially when it takes you away from your family and makes you lose everything that you worked hard for," She noticed how when he said that, he hung his head and that sad look came across his face.

"Oh Trey, I'm sorry. She knew that you were in the Navy. She should have understood that you had to be out working," she said pulling him close and hugging him. She would have understood if she were Julie.

"It is hard on a marriage. Most of the guys that I work with has either gotten divorced or is going through a divorce. The guys leave and the wives can't handle it. A lot of the guys are off cheating when they are away from their wives. I don't blame her because it is very common for a Navy wife to leave. I feel just as bad for the wives as I do the guys. They are stuck at home for months at a time, taking care of the babies while their husbands are out doing what they are told. For the most part, I love my job but then again it can be so hard."

He hugged her back, close to him. She felt the warm wet tears falling onto her shoulder. She hated to see him this hurt. She felt her own tears sliding down her cheeks while she was holding him close caused by the pain that he was feeling. "It is what I chose though. I just kind of wish now that I had made a different decision. She had to uproot her life in Texas and come to me. She did it willingly. She left everything just so she could be with me. Her daughter had to change schools and she had to leave a job and family she loved. I thought she really loved me. If you think about it, she gave everything just to be with me. She left her home, lost her husband for months at a time, and had to lose everything that she knew. I don't blame her for leaving. She did not deserve this life. She never asked for this life. I was the one that asked for this life when I joined the Navy. She never asked to be left alone for months at a time but she accepted it. It was always hard on her. It just got to be too much. This has happened to me twice now Hope. Look at all the Thanksgivings, Christmas Days, birthdays and everything else I missed out on. I lost you because of the distance. I lost both wives because I was out at sea. I realize that as a Navy man, it is not meant for me to be married or in a relationship. No woman deserves that."

"Trey, she knew what she was signing up for when she said I do and signed on the dotted line. She knew that you were military and would be gone for months or maybe even years at a time. She knew that getting you comes with a price. She knew that she would have to leave her home. She accepted it because she did love you. You can't beat yourself up because she messed up. You were Navy before she married you so she knew that you came with a price tag."

"I know but nobody understands how hard it is. Nobody can see how long a few months at sea can feel. She could not have realized until she lived through it. I'm lucky too. There are guys that are deployed in war zones for over a year at a time. I have not had to face that yet. There are guys that come back from those war zones as different guys. Some of them get PTSD and are never the same. They have nightmares, get violent, turn to drugs or alcohol, depression, or often commit suicide. I am lucky, Hope. I have had a really good career if you look at my duty compared to theirs. Tell me Hope, would you be willing to uproot your life and the girls and move to wherever the military decided to send me next? Would you be willing to accept this lifestyle and watch your husband go off for months or years on a submarine, not knowing if he would be coming home or not? What if they shipped us off to Guam or Japan? How would you feel if I went out to sea one day then called you from another country a month later and you never even knew where I was? How would you feel if you were my wife and one day I went to work and never came back home? Don't you think that you would look elsewhere for comfort? Don't you think that you would want to be held when I was gone? It is so easy for the wives to turn to another man. I've had to go through it twice now. We all need to be held and feel loved, Hope. Even I need to be held and to feel loved. I don't blame her at all for any of this. This military life was my choice, not hers."

"Did you cheat on her?"

"No. I can honestly say that I have never cheated on her. She filed for divorce already. The papers are at the base. They have been signed and it is in the process. I am going to miss her and my babies."

"Trey, if I had the opportunity to be in her place and to be your wife I would be willing to move to anywhere we had to go. Yes, I would probably get homesick but you would be worth it. You are and always have been worth waiting for. I would gladly uproot and rearrange my entire life and everything about it to be with you if you were to marry me. I don't understand how she could leave you. You can defend her all you want but I do not understand. I see the prize that she left. I see the gold in you. I would never leave you even if I was never able to see you because I would know that if you could be home with me, you would. You would be off defending me, our kids, and our country. You would be my hero. I could never cheat on you if I had that opportunity. I don't understand how she could have done that. She had the best thing in front of her that she could ever have. You are such a wonderful man, the best friend that anyone could ever ask for, and any girl would be lucky to have you. I know that I was the luckiest girl in the world for the short period of time that I had you." She was speaking the truth.

He pulled her even closer to him and just hugged her as tightly as he could. With tears in his eyes, he leaned down and softly kissed her head tenderly. He said, "Let's go back to your hotel. It's starting to get late."

She reluctantly pulled away from him and started to walk back toward his car. He came up behind her and wrapped his arms around her waist. "Did I tell you how happy I am that you came up here and that I feel like the luckiest guy in the world to have you here with me? I really am Hope."

"Thank you. I am glad."

"I don't know what I would have done without you as my best friend all these years. I have always had you to turn to when I was upset or needed someone. You are amazing. Plus have I told you lately that you are beautiful?"

"Thank you Trey."

"You are still as beautiful now as you were when I went to Breckenridge on my leave and when I first met you when you were in the 8th grade. That leave was the best time of my life. Did I ever tell you that? I think about that weekend all the time. That was the best weekend of my life Hope. Can you believe that? Even better than anything that I ever had with Julie. We had something very special then."

"I think about it every day and I know what you mean. It was the best weekend of my life too. It was really hard to go on after that weekend without you."

"Me too." He said. He was not lying about that. There was not a day that he did not relive those days in his heart. He really loved her and he was so confused about what he wanted. He wanted to be with her so badly but he was still in love with Julie. His heart felt like it was being torn into pieces. He opened the car door for her and then got into the drivers side. He drove her to Wal-Mart then told her that he would be back for her after he grabbed some of his things from the base. I won't be more than 15 minutes or so ok."

She smiled and jumped out of the car and went into the store and got some shampoo, conditioner, and body wash. She decided to order pizza and have it delivered to the hotel. She would call when she got back to the room. After she paid, she walked outside and waited for him to come back. He would be back in a few minutes but a man walked up to her and offered her $25.00 for her services and went into detail on what services that he wanted. He was looking for a hooker. She looked at him and informed him in a very rude voice that she was not a hooker. He popped off about why would she be standing outside if she was not a hooker and walked into the store. That freaked her out so she walked back into Wal-Mart to wait on Trey to come back. Her cell phone rang and it was him saying that he was about to pull into the parking lot and does he need to come in or just pull up to the curb.

"Just pull up to the front and I will get in but hurry up because some man already thought I was a hooker and offered me $25.00 tonight so I came back inside. He scared me."

He started to chuckle and told her that she was worth a lot more than $25.00 and that he didn't understand how he thought was a hooker when she was not even showing cleavage. "Some people are idiots. I'm here." She rushed outside and got into his car and saw him laughing.

"It is not funny," She said pretending to be mad at him.

"I drop you off for 15 minutes without me and you already are getting picked up and hit on. What am I going to do with you," he said, driving off. "Oh I forgot to mention, Charleston has a lot of hookers here so that's probably why he tried to pick you up."

"Really? That's terrible. You are a military man. I know that women throw themselves at you all the time when you are wearing that uniform."

"That is a very good point. The uniform does attract women like a moth to a candle. I never had one offer to pay for it though," he said with his big goofy grin. "Good job."

"Shut up Freshman," she said, smiling. That just made him laugh even harder.

"You know that I am going to give you crap about this for the rest of my life, right?"

"Yep, I would never expect any less," she said and laughed.

They drove back to the hotel and he grabbed his stuff out of the car and she got her Wal-Mart bag full of toiletries. He also grabbed a bottle of wine and brought it in.

"You brought wine? Awesome. That was sweet. I am not much of a drinker but we will enjoy that."

"Yea and I ordered pizza too for supper. They should be here in about 15 minutes. Hope do you still like pepperoni." "You read my mind. I was going to do that too."

"Well, you have spent enough for this trip so I want to pay for the pizza and take you out tomorrow and show you some of the attractions."

"Thanks and pepperoni is still my favorite."

"I know just like me."

"I'm gonna jump in the shower really quick if you don't care. It is pretty humid here." she told him.

"That is fine. I was gonna ask you if I could borrow it too in a little bit. I was working before I picked you up from the airport."

"Of course," she took a quick shower and put her clean clothes on. She was so glad that she was there in that city with him. It was beautiful and she was with the one person that she loved. The feelings had never left her after all these years.

She walked out of the bathroom with a towel around her head and her pajamas on. They were cute but not sexy. He whistled and said, "Dang you sure are beautiful." He gave her a hug, holding her as close as he could. She smelled so good. She was so beautiful and was the sweetest girl that he knew. He pulled away and went into the shower, leaving her the money for pizza.

She was brushing her hair when her phone rang.

"How are things with Mr. Wonderful? I was worried about you so I had to call and check on you. You ready to come home yet?"

"Hey Dean. Things are good. Thank you for calling and checking. You would not believe this place. It is breathtaking. She told him some of the sights that she had seen since she had got there."

"Ok sweetie I'm glad that it is beautiful but that is not why I am calling. How is he treating you? Are you ok? You sound happy. Are you happy? Do you think that you need to call me later for a shoulder to cry on? I will be here right by the phone if you need me."

"Oh no it isn't like that at all. It is wonderful. We are getting along great."

"Are you guys back together?"

"No Dean, I am his friend. That is all we are at this point. He has hugged me and that is about as far as it has gone. He has called me beautiful and he kissed my forehead. He just missed me. That's all."

"I know that you are best friends but the last time you were with that best friend, you spent the entire night, crying your eyes out over him so that is why I am worried."

"It is different now Dean. I am here with him and she is not here. I don't have to see them together. That was kind of like rubbing salt in my wounds. He is here with me so I am not hurt today. I don't know how to explain it. I may need you when I get back though if it is hard to leave or if something does happen and I need a friend though, ok?"

"Yes, of course. I will always be here for you. I pinky promise."

"Hey I will see you when I get back. I am glad you called. I am so thankful to have you as my friend. I don't know what I would do without you. You are a real friend to me Dean." Trey walked out of the bathroom to hear her say the last line. He walked by her, wearing nothing but a towel and grabbed his shorts and underwear off the bed.

"Woops, I forgot," he mouthed silently so she could finish her conversation.

"I'm happy to have you too Hope. Have fun. See when you get back. I'm glad you are enjoying your trip. That makes me very happy. See you when you get back ok. Bye bye."

"Bye."

She could not help but think about how good Trey looked in that towel, with the couple drops of water still running down his back and his wet hair. She hurriedly finished brushing her hair then heard the knock on the door and paid for the pizza.

"So, that was Dean? How has he been? He is a nice guy. Are you guys still pretty close?"

"Yea, he is great. He is there for me."

"Have you ever thought of dating him, Hope? He is really nice and you both seem to get along great? I truly like him as a person. He makes you laugh also and I love that about him. He even made me laugh. He is a very funny guy."

"Oh no. He is just a friend. He is kind of like a brother. He is getting married soon. He's going to have a baby. We have never been involved romantically?"

"Really wow, I hope his marriage works out. You hungry?"

"Starving. You get the pizza and I will pour our wine into these little plastic fancy hotel cups," she said smiling at the only cups they had in the room. He grinned really big.

They sat there eating and talked for hours. "Hope, when you think about that weekend, what do you think about? Do you regret it?"

"You know what, I would never regret that weekend Trey. I was happier that weekend than I have ever been in my entire life. Honestly, I think about what could have been and what if. I question what happened to us because it felt so real. I wonder if it was all a game to you or just a act to get me in bed with you. I don't think it was though because you could not have faked those emotions. I remember you looking into my eyes, singing Good Morning Beautiful to me and about the first moment you kissed me. I think about every second of it. I think about how you flew into town and surprised me. I think about that tear that fell down your cheek when you had to leave me. Trey that was real. Nobody has ever done anything like that. I could never regret it in my lifetime. Do you ever regret it?"

"No way, Hope and I was never just about getting you in bed with me. Hope I had liked you since I was in seventh grade. I had always wanted a chance with you. I don't know what happened. I wanted to make the relationship work but how was it going to work when I was over a thousand miles away. Hope the Navy kept us apart. I knew that you had your daughters and it was not fair to ask you to uproot them and take them away from Seth, your parents, and their lives. I thought about all that. I had requested a transfer to Texas but they would not let me have it. If you had flown up to Hawaii to see me when you planned on coming, I was going to surprise you with a ring though. You never came and that does not make me mad but then I met Julie and fell in love with her before I could get to you."

"I can't believe that you were going to give me a ring?"

"I was."

She felt the tears filling her eyes and spilling over onto her face. "I'm so sorry I never came to see you. I wanted to so badly."

"Don't cry sweetie. Everything happens for a reason. If I had married you, I would have never had my son and I love my son. I have one question though. Would you have said yes?"

"Yes," she said, still crying.

"Hey don't cry ok. I like seeing your beautiful smile. He pulled her close and kissed her tear. She threw her arms around him and pulled him even closer. He leaned in and kissed her softly on the lips. She kissed him back. They laid in the bed kissing for a long time then she pulled away.

"I can't do this. You are still in love with Julie. I don't want to have to get over you twice. It would kill both of us."

"Hope, there is nobody on earth that I would rather be with than you right this second. I am not even thinking of Julie. I just want to be with you. I have been crazy about you for 15 years now. We are getting divorced hon. The papers will be filed soon. I want to be with you Hope. I need you to kiss me please."

"Please don't make me regret this."

"Do you regret the weekend? No. Why on earth would you ever regret this weekend?"

"I never regretted it Trey but it killed me seeing you with another woman that was not me."

"It also killed me knowing that you got remarried sweetie. They are not important now. All that matters is you and I right now."

She kissed him again. They made love again and held each other the rest of the night. Her hopes were high. She could not wait to start their lives together now. That had to be what this moment meant. She was so excited and full of emotion. It felt so good to be in his arms again. She needed him so badly. They were going to be such a wonderful couple. They were going to be so happy together. If he were to ask her to move to be with him, she would do it right then. If he only knew how happy she was right then, he would have asked her on the spot. They fell asleep in each others arms and she slept like a baby being wrapped up in him. He was laying there thinking about how he was the luckiest man alive right then. He loved her so much and needed her. He thought about asking her to move to be with him but thought that he would surprise her and request another transfer to Texas and maybe she would not have to leave her home to come to him when he would be going out to sea all the time anyway. He lay there watching her sleep so peacefully, thinking about how he could possibly make this work. He wanted that night to last forever but like all nights, the morning arrived.

The next morning she was the first to wake up. She lay there watching him sleep. He looked so peaceful. She noticed that even in his sleep he was smiling. She smiled. She didn't dare move because she did not want to wake him. His alarm went off after awhile and he seen her watching him sleep.

He looked at her and started to sing *Good Morning Beautiful* to her. She felt happy tears welling up in her eyes. She was the luckiest girl alive right then. After he finished singing, she kissed his forehead and he pulled her to him to kiss her on the lips even though she knew that her morning breath probably smelled like something dead.

"You ready to get up and go see Charleston?"

"Do we really have to get out of bed?" she asked.

He grinned from ear to ear. "I would be perfectly content staying in bed with you for the rest of our lives but you came all the way down here and you need to enjoy Charleston. Come on sweetie. Let's get up. I have to be at work at 4." They got dressed then went to have breakfast and went to the beach. She took another picture of them in front of the water. He spent the rest of the day taking her around the city then explained that he was going to have to go to get her back to the hotel so he could go to work. "I am so sorry."

"Trey it is your job. It is ok."

"I will drop you off and I will come back to you tonight ok. I get off at midnight so I should be back around 12:30 or so ok?"

"Sounds great," she told him.

He took her back to the hotel. He walked her to her hotel room and went in and put on his uniform.

"See you later sweetheart. Thank you again for understanding my job. Thank you so much for coming to see me baby."

"I can't wait until you get back."

"Well, you have the pool and you can always get a cab if you want to go do something. Do you need cab fare?"

"No I have money. Awesome. Thanks for everything Trey."

He leaned in and kissed her again. "See you tonight Beautiful. I am by far the luckiest man alive right now. Be careful around here and don't go find you a pimp while I am gone," he said chuckling.

"Shut up," she said grinning from ear to ear.

They told each other bye again and kissed each other one last time before he walked away. She decided that she would take advantage of this beautiful city and call a cab. The cab driver was very nice and offered to come back to pick her up after she was ready to go back to the hotel and gave her his cell phone number. She decided to take a carriage ride around the city so she could learn even more than he had already told her. Her driver was telling her about the history of slavery and how his ancestors had owned slaves back in the day and how after they were freed, many of the slaves they had chose to stay and work for them. He explained that as he was growing up, one of their descendants was his Mammy which was the lady that watched him when his mother was busy and also took care of the house. His Mammy still worked for his family to that day. She saw more beautiful sights and truly enjoyed herself. She walked down the beautiful rock road. She walked a few blocks and found a restaurant that the carriage driver had recommended. As she was eating, her phone rang and it was Trey. "Hi beautiful. I was just calling to check on you. Is everything alright?"

"Yes I just sitting down to supper and then I will call the cab driver back to come get me in a little bit." She told him about her day and the activities that she had done. He apologized again for having to leave her by herself and she told him not to worry about it. They said goodbye and hung up. She ate some supper then decided that it was time to return to the hotel so when she was finishing her meal, she called the cab driver and told him to meet her at the harbor in front of the bridge where she was headed back to.

"So what brings you to Charleston," the cabbie asked her.

"I came to see my best friend. He is in the Navy and stationed here."

"Wow, where are you from?"

"Breckenridge, Texas."

"I never heard of Breckenridge. Where is that by?" She smiled because she heard that often. She explained that it was an hour from Abilene. He said, "Wow, you have come a long way to see a guy best friend. Any chance of a relationship? How long are you in town for? You interested in moving down here?"

"Yes. Hopefully he will be my boyfriend soon. I really want that and if he asked me to, I would be here in a heartbeat. I flew down for the weekend. He had to work tonight but will be back later."

"Wow, I wish you guys the best. You seem like a nice girl. I hope that it works out. I love a happy ending."

"Me too. Thank you sir," she told him when he pulled up the hotel, handing him the money. "If I need a ride to the airport, I will give you a call ok."

"Sounds good. Thank you."

"Thank you Sir." She went into the room and decided to take a dip in the pool before he got back and before they closed the pool down. Everyone was so nice. As she was swimming, several guys talked to her that was sitting outside of their hotel room. A guy named Randy came down as she was swimming and started a conversation with her. He was asking where she was from and why she was in town. They talked about Trey and he was a very nice guy. She told him goodbye after the hotel supervisor locked it up.

"Nice meeting you Randy. Everyone is so nice here."

"Well, you are a pretty lady so everyone is going to be nice."

"Thank you. Enjoy the rest of your stay," she told him.

"Hey, I have a bottle of wine at my hotel. How about we open it up and drink it together until your friend gets back."

"I don't think that is such a good idea. I would not do anything to make him mad and plus I am hoping that we are back together. Plus I don't know you enough to go into your hotel room."

"Ok, how about this then. We can sit on the hotel steps outside, drinking the wine and just get to know one another. We have until Midnight and it is only 9. You can go back to Texas and tell everyone that you to met a man from Missouri when you went to South Carolina. That would be cool. I don't know anyone from Texas and I think your accent is cute."

"Sure as long as you understand that we are never going to be anything more than friends and I am not going to bed with you."

"What? Why on earth would I want to take you to bed? I'm a nice guy but if you insist," he said laughing. They both started to laugh. They talked for awhile about her family, his family, and the job he was doing. He told her that he had not seen the bridge that she was talking about and he probably would not get the opportunity because he was leaving at 6AM to go to Ohio for another job so he would not have the time. After talking for a couple of hours, she told him that he was going to have to leave so that she could take a shower before Trey got back. They both enjoyed the visit. "Ok sweetheart but before I leave, can I do one thing?" He leaned forward and tried to kiss her. She pulled her head away and reminded him that she was in love with Trey.

"Ok then I understand. Good luck with him. Hope it works out for you. Can I please give you a hug and get your number so we can keep in touch? I would like to stay friends if that is cool and maybe one day I will go to work in Texas." When she shook her head yes, he leaned over and hugged her bye. He programmed her phone number into his phone. He walked away and went to his hotel room. As she was about to get into the shower her phone rang. It was a strange number but she answered it because it could be Trey calling from work. "Hey, I was just checking to make sure you gave me the right number." She laughed and told him that she would not give him the wrong number and they both laughed. "Ok talk to you later." She got in the shower and then put her clean sexy nightgown that she had packed just in case. She brushed her hair then laid down on the bed to watch some television. Tomorrow would be her last day there and she knew that it would kill her once again to leave there without him. That thought reminded her that is what it will be like if they do ever get married. He will have to sometimes leave her for months or possibly years at a time. She thought about how hard it would be to be a military wife but remembered right away that he was worth it and how amazing it would be to wake up everyday for the rest of their lives in each others arms. She thought about the how exciting it would be every time that he came home. She thought about how amazing it would be to have him come back and see him get off that plane and run into her arms and them be a family again. She thought about the fact that one day when he goes out, he may never return. Soldiers know when they leave that they may never come home and so do their wives. Could she handle that? He was worth every single heartache that she would have to face because she would know that he would be coming home to her. If he did have to give up his life, she would die knowing that he wanted to be with her in his final hours. She fell asleep after laying there for a little while.

    She was awaken to someone crawling into bed with her. "It's just me," he told her quietly. "I'm sorry. I was not able to get off on time so it is 3AM."

    "It's ok. I know that there will be times that I will have to wait even longer for you to come home if I was to be with you."

    "Baby, thank you so much for being such a sweetheart." She kissed him and they kissed for awhile and made love again. "I don't want you to leave tomorrow. I wish that you could stay."

"I could come back if you want me to but I have to finish up some things and would need to get my clothes and stuff."

"You would really move here for me?"

"Yes."

"I must be the luckiest guy alive." He meant every word that he said. He truly believed those words when he said them. The next morning, she climbed out of bed and started to get her things together. She had a flight at 8AM. He was just going to be able to get her to the airport before he had to be at work. She brushed her teeth so he would not smell her morning breath again and finished packing. After she packed herself, she packed the rest of his stuff in his bag for him. He woke up and looked at his watch.

"Crap, I overslept."

"I got your stuff packed and I already packed mine so everything is ready to go. You can keep the shampoo and stuff. It is easier than taking it on the plane."

He smiled as he pulled his uniform on. "Thank you for packing my stuff. He quickly brushed his teeth and came back in and kissed her. "I am going to miss you so much. This weekend was amazing."

"I know and I will miss you too. Thank you for everything."

He pulled her close and wanted to just keep holding her but knew that they had to get gone. "Come on sweetheart. We have to go." She decided to just hang onto her hotel key. They would not miss it and it was another memory of him to her. He grabbed his bag then hers as well and took them out to the car. He tossed them into the trunk and drove to the airport. He got out of the car, grabbed her bag, and they both started to bawl. They both knew that this was going to be hard to leave one another again. "Dream about me ok sweetheart. I promise to dream about you. Remember that song "I'm Already There because I will be there for you even though we are physically away from each other," he told her.

"Ok you dream about me too ok. I will come back. I want to be with you forever."

"I promise. See you soon beautiful." He kissed her one last time and she turned to walk into the airport, bawling until the plane landed on the ground in Dallas. In Dallas, she grabbed her bag and loaded it into her car to drive to Galveston. She shot him a quick text letting him know that she had made it back in Dallas. She was going to meet her family on vacation and have a good time with them but would she be able to make it again and go on without him? She knew that if she just thought about how she was going to make it happen to move down there that she would make it and that gave her strength. He did something that he had not done the entire time that he had been enlisted. He drove back to the barracks and called rank to tell them that he was sick and was not going to be at work that day. He was not physically sick but his heart was. He was sure going to miss her. He laid on his bed and just bawled his eyes out. Even though that was the second best weekend of his life, it was harder to let her go the second time than it was the first. It killed his heart watching her leave again. On her way to Galveston, she called Dean because she knew that he would be on his way to work.

"Hey Hope. How was your weekend?"

"Dean, it was amazing. I plan on trying to get the money together and move here soon. We are back together. I am so happy."

He felt his heart sink. He really didn't understand why because he wanted her to be happy but he was scared that she had just been played. He wasn't going to tell her that though. He didn't have it in his heart to break her heart.

"That's great Hope. Do you know how long it will take you guys to move over there? I sure am going to miss you."

"I don't know but it was the best weekend of my life Dean. It was just as wonderful as the first one. I can't even compare them because they were both so special so I will just say that I have had the best weekend of my life twice now. I am so happy."

"Hope, I am thrilled for you. You deserve to be happy and I hope that this guy treats you like you deserve to be treated. You are special Hope so don't let him treat you any less."

"I wouldn't Dean. He wouldn't. You know him. He is a sweetheart."

"Oh I know. I liked him a lot. Well Hope if you are happy, I am happy for you. I am up here at work though sweetie so I will holler at you later ok? I am always here for you no matter what even if he frowns on our friendship."

"Oh he don't care. He heard you and I talking on the phone when you called. He met you the one day that I brought you to South Texas with me to meet them. Trust me, he is fine with it."

"Wow, moving to South Carolina. I truly did not know that you had it in you Hope. I am happy for you. Talk to you later. Have fun in Galveston with your family."

"Thanks Dean. Bye."

"Bye," he hung up the phone but was really worried about her. She sure had her hopes up for this guy that lived a thousand miles away. He sure had his doubts but didn't want to see her when she came to him to hold her up through it because he already knew how hard she would take it when it happened. She was going to be devastated if it didn't work out. He believed in his heart that it would not work out.

She had a wonderful time with her family through the rest of the week. She enjoyed hanging around on cloud 9 for awhile because it felt so good to be up there. She had never been that happy in her entire life and could not wait to start a life with him.

It felt like her life was going to end approximately a week later when she got the text. "I am really struggling now. I am lost and trying to find myself. I will call you when I can talk but right now I just need some time for myself and time to think. Hope I am sorry but right now I just am not sure what I want. I am still in love with her and have not healed and now I have probably thrown away our friendship. Please forgive me. I will get back to you when I can." Her heart sank and she felt as if the breath had just been knocked out of her. Is this really happening? Was he going to go back to her after the weekend that they just spent together? She did not understand. He was happy. He wanted to be with her. Now she not only was going to lose her boyfriend again but was once again going to have to lose her best friend.

Through the tears she texted him back. "I am sorry that you are lost. You were my friend first so you know that I will always be here for you when you are ready to talk or reach out to me. Trey I want you to know that I will be praying that God's will to be done in your life. If she is what makes you happy, I hope you can get back with her because despite everything I only want to see you happy. If someone else is the one that will make you happy, I only want that for you. My phone will always be on."

That would be the last time that she would hear from him for years. Amelia and Dean was busy listening to her cry for years. She leaned on them for her strength because she did not have it. It had felt like Trey had picked her up and broke her into a million pieces. If waiting on him was all that she could do then she would have to do it.

# Chapter 11

## This Can't be Real

One day about 2 years later Mitzi Boggs knocked on her door. Her girls were at school. Hope had been waiting on Trey to call her for just over 2 years but the call never came. She had texted him a few times throughout those years but he never responded to her efforts. She had seen one day on Facebook that he came to Breckenridge and did not even bother to come see her. She did not understand. She had flown all the way across country to see him and he couldn't even bother to pick up the phone and call when he was in town? Why had he dumped her? She could handle losing the boyfriend again. She had been through it before but not the best friend. She had a friend from work call him when he was in town and ask who she had called, pretending to have gotten a wrong number and it was still Trey's phone number so he was choosing to ignore her. She had to know if he had changed his phone number. She was certain that he must have or he would have answered at least one text but it was still his number. Her heart had sank again when she found out that it was him so he had kept the same number but would not respond to her calls. Why would he do this to her?

"Hey Hope, have you looked at Trey's Facebook page today? If you haven't, I think that there is something you should know."

"No what's up? Is he in Breckenridge again and still ignoring me? That's about right," she said sarcastically. She was so tired of him ignoring her and could not hide her sarcasm any longer.

"Um no not exactly. I don't want to tell you this because it is going to kill you but he got married again. I'm sorry you had to hear it from me."

"What? He got married again? I have not even dated anyone since him and he has already gotten married? Mitzi, are you messing with me?"

"No, I would not hurt you like that on purpose. I'm sorry. There's something else. He put a picture of them when he started dating her it looks like he may have been dating her when you went to Charleston or he started right after you left. I am so sorry to have to tell you this. I am so mad at him right now."

"Ok Mitzi, you did not have to tell me that!" she said, emphasizing the word not. "I really did not want to hear either of them but I think the fact that he may have had a girlfriend then is worse than him getting married. He did not act like he had a girlfriend then. How do you know the date?"

"They had a picture of them from when they first met and it had the date on the picture. It was next to their wedding picture as a before and after. Hope, are you ok?"

"No, he had moved on a week after that amazing weekend? Mitzi, am I really that easy to forget?"

"No Hope, I don't understand it. I do not understand it or him."

"I don't either. This is just not possible." She felt the tears filling her eyes and spilling over onto her face. "Mitzi. Why can't I get past him? Why do I have to love him? I have not moved on since 2001. Mitzi, it has been 9 years that I have loved him. You didn't see him that weekend. He was so happy. Do you think he was seeing her too when I went down there? You also did not see him when he came in on leave and surprised me. How the hell do you fake that? Those feelings he had were real. At least they looked real. No they were real. If they were not real, he would have never cried about me in front of his ex wife. They had to be real."

"Hope, I honestly don't know. He looked pretty cozy with her in the picture from that day. Have you even went on one date since that day?"

"No, I have been completely faithful even though he would not talk to me. I know that it don't make sense but I refused to give up on him. I decided to wait on him and I have been doing it since I got home. Mitzi, can you please just let me cry on you?"

"Come here." Hope broke. All the emotions, feelings, and tears that she had been hanging onto for the past two years came crashing down on her again. She cried for hours.

"Mitzi, I am sorry but I kind of just need to be left alone ok."

"Sorry friends don't do that. I am here for you and I am not going anywhere."

All of a sudden, she was filled with an overwhelming sense of rage. "That sorry sack of crap. He used me. He just used me for sex. He never felt anything but he knew that if he made me believe that he did that I would do it with him because my feeling were so real. Right now I hate him. He has done that to me twice now. He never really cared for me. He was faking just to get what he wanted. He screwed up my head just so he could get pleasure." She felt the sadness and confusion coming back to her. "How do you fake that Misty? How do you force yourself to cry? Why would he waste his time calling me everyday for months? Why would he introduce me to his family and make me his son's Godmother if the feelings were not real? I don't understand. Was this some test that I miserably failed? I can't do this. I can't face this. I just want to hit him right now. He deserves to be hit right in the face. I hate him."

"Hope, you don't hate him. You are hurt and you are angry. You feel like you have suffered, waiting on him this entire time so he should have waited on you as well. You are angry. He just yanked the rug out from in under your dreams, your hopes, and your heart. What you are feeling is normal. Do I think that he was faking? No. I think the boy had true feelings for you. I think that he was in love with you. You could see it on his face. You can see it in your pictures with him. If he was just after sex, he would have dumped you right after he got it, not called you daily for months afterwards. He daggum sure would have never made you his son's Godmother. Hope, I don't know. This don't make any sense at all to me. Maybe he chose her because she was there. You would have to leave everything to be with him. He knows that. She was easier to be with than you. She probably was what got him through his divorce. Hope, you have to move on now. You deserve to be happy too. I know a lot of guys over the past couple years that would have treated you great but you were too busy wanting to be with him. You have ultimately hurt yourself more by waiting on him. You know how much I loved Mason in high school, right? I loved him with everything inside me but I broke his heart. He was good to me. He did not deserve that."

"Why did you do it then? Why did Trey do this to me Mitzi? I did not deserve it either. Help me understand. Mitzi, I have to try to calm down. The girls will be home before long and will want to know why I have been crying." She tried splashing water on her face and running the fan to see if that would help but her face still resembled a tomato.

"I was scared to death Hope. I was scared because I loved him too much. I was not ready to be in love with anyone and it was easier to just let him go than to stay with him with those feelings. Mason did not deserve to be hurt. He was a wonderful guy. You know, I loved him more than I have ever loved anyone in my entire life. That day that you and I ran into him, it was so hard on me, Hope. I wanted to get back with him so bad but I can't. I can't ever go back now. It is too late for him and me. He never got married. I have looked him up on Facebook a thousand times but I won't add him. It is too dangerous, Hope. I know that if I ever crossed a certain line with him, I could never go back and that is not fair to the guy I am with now. He is good to me and don't deserve to be hurt so I can't ever talk to Mason again. I know that it is just too dangerous. He was my best friend for a long time also Hope. Hope, have you ever thought that maybe Trey believes the most caring thing that he can do is to not talk to you. He knows that he loves you and he knows that you love him. He knows that Julie could sense the connection between you and him and he is worried that will happen to him again. He realizes that it was cruel for y'all to stay friends with those kinds of feelings. Maybe he realizes that it would kill you to see him with another woman again. Maybe he just had to move on Hope. You have to let him go now. Mason had to let me go and he never deserved it, just like you did not deserve it. I want to apologize to you. I am apologizing to you for every scared person who could not commit to the person that they loved. I can't apologize to Mason, so I am apologizing to you for Trey because I did the same thing."

"I just don't understand. I was willing to stay friends with him even though it hurt. I loved him that much and I did not want to lose him but now I have had to."

"Hope, the kindest thing for Mason was for me to let him go. Trying to stay friends hurt both of us more than either of us deserved. I think that is why he just dropped you, sweetie. He just could not stand to see you with someone else and did not want to tell you the truth about him seeing someone else. He knew that it would be easier to just let you go and not speak to you than to see you hurt. He could not stand to hurt you so he let you go so he would not have to see it or thought maybe that it would be easier on you. You need to forgive him sweetie. Forgive him not because he deserves it but forgive him so you can move on. You deserve the opportunity to move on without him in your life."

"How would you know that Mitzi?"

"Because that is how I felt about Mason and because I asked him what happened and why he just let your friendship die. I am sorry. I understand if you are mad at me but you deserved to know. I was mad at him for doing that to you. I hope one day you can forgive me. Trey was sorry and he still loves you to this day. He was trying to be kind. He told me that. He has loved you for years but being with you hurt him. He said that it was like having your favorite food in front of you but you could not touch it."

"When did you ask him that Mitzi?"

"Today after I saw his wedding pictures. He said that he had sent you a message on Facebook about a year ago, trying to help you to see why he had done it because it was not fair to you. He told me that you never answered the message and he thought you didn't answer because you were mad at him for just walking away. He said that he could not stand to see you hurting anymore. He said that he could not stand to be hurt anymore. He said that he was not going to allow you to uproot your life and move a thousand miles away like he did his ex because eventually she resented him for that and he didn't want you to ever resent him."

"What? I never got a message from him. He has not spoken to me in about 2 years."

"If I were you, I would go back and look at your messages again because he swears that he sent you one. He may be lying, but I don't think he is. I think he truly sent one or he typed it out and forgot to hit send."

"Ok, I will but I swear he did not send me anything on Facebook lately. Is she good to him Mitzi? Does she treat him the way that he deserves to be treated? Why didn't you tell me that he was getting married? Truthfully I love him so much that all I ever wanted was for him to be happy."

"I didn't know and yes she is really good to him. She had 2 little babies and he loves them. She loves his baby. He is happy. I know you always wanted him to be happy. I saw that when he was with Julie. You were willing to put your own feelings aside so that he could have the opportunity to be happy. He knows that too but didn't want to see you have to do it again."

Hope smiled. "Good. I truly hope that they last forever because all I ever wanted was for him to be happy. Now let's go look at this picture of them so I can see who he married."

Together they looked at his page and saw that he had married a really cute brunette with a huge smile. He looked so happy in his pictures with her so Hope was happy for him. She had always been willing to put her feelings on the back burner so that he would have a chance to be happy. She looked at her messages and there was not anything in her main folder from him but she noticed that there was a letter in her other folder from him. She opened it and it was just the words to a song that he had typed out. He always had hated boy bands so the fact that he took the time to listen to a song from a boy band and type the words out for her really hit her hard. The letter was dated over a year ago. How had it gotten lost in cyber space for over a year? The letter simply said the words to the song and a quick explanation. After she read it, she finally felt a sense of peace. The tears fell down her cheeks but they were not tears of pain. They were tears of understanding and tears of forgiveness. He really had loved her. It was not all in her head. She finally understood. She had needed that closure and thankfully it had finally come.

"Mitzi, as weird as this sounds, I finally feel like I can move on. That weight has finally been lifted."

### ***The Hardest Thing***

By: 98 Degrees

> We both know that I shouldn't be here
> This is wrong
> And baby it's killing me
> It's killing you
> Both of us trying to be strong
> I've got somewhere else to be
> Promises to keep
> Someone else who loves me
> And Trusting me fast asleep
> I've made up my mind
> There is no turning back
> She's been good to me
> And she deserves better than that.

It's the hardest thing I'll ever had to do
To look you in the eye and tell you I don't love you
It's the hardest thing I'll ever have to lie
To show no emotion when you start to cry
I can't let you see what you mean to me
When my hands are tied and my hearts not free
We're not meant to be
It's the hardest thing I'll ever have to do
To turn around and walk away
Pretending I don't love you.

I know we'll meet again
Fate has a place and time
So you can get on with your life
I've got to be cruel to be kind
Like Doctor Zhivago
All my love I'll be sending
And you will never know
Cause there can be no happy ending.

It's the hardest thing I'll ever have to do
To look you in the eye and tell you I don't love you
It's the hardest thing I'll ever have to lie
To show no emotion when you start to cry
I can't let you see what you mean to me
When my hands are tied and my heart's not free
We're not meant to be.
It's the hardest thing I'll ever have to do
To turn around and walk away
Pretending I don't love you

Maybe another time, another day
As much as I want to I can't stay
I've made up my mind
There is no turning back
She's been good to me
And she deserves better than that.

## When Forever Fails

It's the hardest thing I'll ever have to do
To look you in the eye and tell you I don't love you
It's the hardest thing I'll ever have to lie
To show no emotion when you start to cry
I can't let you see what you mean to me
When my hands are tied and my heart's not free
We're not meant to be
It's the hardest thing I'll ever have to do
To turn around and walk away pretending I don't love you.
You know I can't do it babe
Don't wanna live a lie.
What can I do
Oh baby oh baby.

I'm sorry Hope. I hope you can forgive me one day. I have to walk away from you for us both to move on. I will always cherish what we had but it is not fair for either of us to have to put our lives on hold or you to have to uproot your life for me. It's not fair to your for the girls. Please find it in your heart to forgive me one day. We will always have the leave and Charleston. Those weekends were not just weekends for me. They were the best weekends of my life. I will always love you, Hope.

Trey

## Chapter 12

## *Life Begins Again*

That was the day that Hope began living again. She started going on dates, spending time having fun again, and just decided that she was going to live for her and her daughters only. She did not have anyone special in her life but had decided that she really didn't need a guy anymore. She was finally able to forgive Trey and understood why he had turned away from her. She even forgave Seth for the years of abuse that he has put her through and they were able to talk and actually get along good for the most part again. She had never thought that would ever be possible. He had remarried and had 3 babies of his own after their divorce. She did not wish anything bad on either of them. She had not spoken to Tim for years so didn't know what was going on in his world but she had also forgiven him as well and herself for not putting more of a fight into trying to save their marriage when he had pulled away from her. She had written him a letter asking him to forgive her for not working harder on their marriage. She told him that she did not want that relationship back, but she wanted to ask him to forgive her. One of her really good friends had sent her on a Walk

To Emmaus and that had really helped her to find forgiveness and fill the void that she had in her heart for so long.

She rededicated her life to God, which filled the Jesus sized hole that men had left in her heart over the years. She lived for God now and wanted to spend the rest of her life serving Him. Looking back, she was thankful for the friendship that she had made with Trey but even more thankful that he had finally had the courage to let her go. She realized that God sent people into each other's lives when they needed them the most and she had needed him when she was going through the divorce with Seth. She needed him to show her how it felt to be loved and for a guy to be nice to her. He had been in her life for a reason but the time had come to let each other go. She understood that now. As bad as it had hurt her at the time, she now could see that the kindest thing that he could have ever done for her was to let her go.

After many years, he would occasionally send her a message asking how she was doing on Facebook and she would let him know and find out about his family as well but they never got too deep with their conversations anymore. He was planning on retiring from the Navy after 20 years and that time was approaching fast. All his pictures on Facebook showed a very happy family so that made her happy. He had been her rock, her best friend, and he deserved the utmost happiness in the world. Truthfully she had never wanted anything but that for him so seeing it left her heart full of gladness.

Her daughters had grown into beautiful young ladies and she had actually became a grandmother to the two most gorgeous little girls that ever walked the face of the earth. She met those babies and was reminded what true love was actually about. Having children is a wonderful experience, but grandbabies have a special tug at their grandma's heart that is unexplainable.

Dean and his wife had separated and she was able to be the rock that he needed while going through that separation. She was there for him while he broke down and cried to her the same way that he had been her rock through Trey. She realized that no matter what, she always had a true friend in him and was thankful for that even though they both accepted the fact that they were just meant to be friends only.

They had been there for one another for years. She was bound and determined to never allow anything to screw up that friendship for them and so was he. She was patiently waiting on God to deliver the one that he had chosen for her because when you rely on God and you believe with everything inside of you, He will never let you down. He would bring her the Nicholas Sparks character she had always dreamed of that would be worth waiting for. If he didn't bring that to her, she was happy with the life she had been given. She was truly happier than she had been in years.

"Hey, you ready to go to Abilene, Hope?"

"Sure but I get to pick the music," she said, grinning. She loved to tease him about that.

"I brought my 80s rock for us to listen to because I know we can compromise on that and we won't have to listen to country," he said shaking his head and smiled at her really big. He had his 2 beautiful babies by his side and they were about to go to Chuck E Cheese in Abilene and have some fun together. His oldest daughter had grown into a beautiful young lady as well and had given birth to her first baby. They had dated each other after his divorce and even though they had a good time together when they dated, they both agreed that all they could ever be is really good friends.

"Ok truce." They gave each other a hug and headed out the door to go to Abilene to have a great time together. He would make her laugh the entire time, like he always had. She loved his babies and helped them into the car and listened to them chattering nonstop in the back seat of his car. Spending time with his kids reminded her of her babies when they were younger. She loved the sound of children.

As they were walking to the restaurant, she glanced up to the sky and told God thank you for being next to her through all her trials, tribulations, and temptations. She silently thanked him for allowing her to go through everything that she had been through because every single valley and mountaintop helped to create who she is today. She now had strength that she never thought was possible. She had someone in the front seat of her life that was driving her around who would never let her down. That special somebody was God. With God all things are possible and he gives you a joy that you would otherwise never have or understand. He had helped her to find forgiveness she never knew possible. He had healed her and set her free.

She had booked a cruise and crossed many items off her bucket list with more waiting on her to fulfill. She had swam with dolphins, gone on beautiful vacations, and spent many nights hanging out with her wonderful family and friends. She truly could not ask for more than the life that she had. She served God as often as she had the chance, which also made her happy. She was planning on going on a mission trip in 2018 to help others who were less fortunate than her. As far as she was concerned, her life was just beginning and she had a wonderful future ahead of her. It took her losing her forever to realize that forever had just begun. Forever may fail you, but when you stop and open your eyes, you realize that the alternate path laid out before you may just be better than the forever you had planned for yourself.